EMERALD MAN

LEIGH STEPHENS

Editors: Judith Cook, Carol Nichols
Cover design: Chris Lorenzen

ISBN:0692982795
ISBN 13: 9780692982792

Courage is being scared to death but saddling up anyway
--John Wayne--

Table of Contents

Prologue

The young woman heard approaching horses and hastened her step as she ran over the rough terrain. Exhausted and out of breath, she stumbled on rocks and tufts of grass, desperate for a place to hide.

"They're coming," she mumbled.

Holding her aching side, she searched the horizon and not finding a place to rest, had no choice but to keeping moving toward the looming hills ahead.

"You got no place to hide girlie," a man shouted in an ominous voice as the horses drew near.

"Let her go," a second man called. "She ain't gonna hurt us now."

Reaching a hill, the young woman frantically climbed, falling to the hard ground on her hands and knees. Rising, she continued to push toward the crest.

"Shoot her now," the first man called. "Before she gets to the top or you'll be running up there after her."

The sound of a single gunshot echoed through the hills. The woman felt a stabbing pain in her shoulder and gasped for air. Tumbling to the ground, her head struck a boulder. She rolled down the hill, stopping at the feet of the horses.

The early morning sun was blinding as the woman stared through blurry vision at the men on horseback. "Run, they're coming," she murmured.

"Check to see if she's dead."

A cloudy form climbed from the saddle, squatted next to her and touching two fingers to the side of her neck, felt for a pulse. The woman opened her eyes and tried to speak.

"Shhh, don't move," he whispered in a voice barely audible. He put his hands over her eyes and shut them, stood up, and walked back to his horse. "She's gone."

The young woman lay there, eyes closed, listening as horses galloped off. Her head was bursting with pain as blood ran down the side of her face. She moaned and touched her shirt, drenched from the gunshot wound. I'm dying, she thought as everything went dark.

CHAPTER 1

LEFT FOR DEAD

Nevada 1878

Griffin Kelly looked at the tracks he'd picked up a few miles back. Two, maybe three horses had passed this way within the last couple of hours. Someone besides him must be looking for that cougar. It wasn't surprising considering most of the ranchers in the area were losing stock.

He looked toward the hills in the distance and moved his horse forward, following the tracks on the ground. It might be a couple of wranglers just passing through, he thought, looking around pensively at the barren land and sighing deeply. These hills were isolated and dangerous for a man alone. He hadn't ruled out the idea that the tracks belonged to rustlers. The last thing Griffin wanted was to run into trouble alone in these hills.

"What is that?" he muttered, spotting a form lying at the base of the hill. His gut told him whatever it was hadn't been killed by an animal. Pulling his rifle from the scabbard and looking around once more, he pointed his horse in that direction. When he drew closer he recognized the form as human and quickened his pace, listening intently for sounds that might signal someone else was near. He cautiously climbed down and knelt beside the body.

The girl's ashen face was covered in dirt as Griffin brushed her matted hair to the side with his hand. Blood trickled down her cheek. Her skin was clammy and rolling her over, he found a bullet wound.

"I think it's safe to say those riders weren't hunting a cougar, Rascal." The horse shook his head as if to agree. Grabbing a canteen, he pulled a handkerchief from his back pocket and soaked it with water. "I say we load her up and get out of here before they decide to come back. This place is starting to give me the creeps."

The young woman moved with a startled jerk when the cold, wet scarf touched her head. She moaned slightly and tried to brush Griffin's hand away. "Careful," he said softly. "I don't want you tearing that shoulder up any more than it already is." He pressed the cloth against the bullet wound. "Jeez, who did this to you?"

The woman opened her eyes, staring blankly as Griffin raised her head and dribbled water over her parched lips. "How did you get all the way out here?" he asked, holding the canteen to her mouth. "Anyone else besides me realize you're still alive?"

"They're coming," she whispered, struggling to get up.

"That's what I'm afraid of," said Griffin, picking her up and setting her in the saddle. He mounted his horse holding the woman tight in his arms and gently nudged the animal forward. "Let's head home."

Rascal's slow, methodical pace wasn't covering much ground but with the girl's gunshot wound it was dangerous to go faster. Griffin didn't think she had much chance of surviving no matter how slow they went. Her breathing was shallow and leaning against his chest she was as limp as a rag. The woman moaned, wincing in pain as Rascal stumbled on a rock. "Hang on, we're almost there."

He pulled her dark hair back hoping to recognize her face. "Where did you come from?" he asked but the woman mumbled incoherently. He thought again of the tracks he saw close to where he found her. They headed east up through the hills. He hoped whoever made them was long gone. Anyone who would shoot a woman and leave her to die was trouble and impossible to catch unless this girl woke up with an explanation for what happened.

Adjusting his weight in the saddle, Griff clutched the girl's waist as he rode up to the house where a gray-haired man paced back and forth on the porch. Jesse was Griff's ranch hand and not pleased with Griff's idea of heading out early that morning to look for a cougar. He was missing calves and so far, the only explanation was the mountain lions that haunted the foothills. Griff didn't much like the idea himself. He usually hunted with his brother but circumstances didn't allow for that today so he went alone. He knew Jesse wouldn't rest comfortably until he returned and grimaced at the thought of what might have happened to this girl if he had stayed home. He watched Jesse reach for the woman without saying a word as he let her slide off his horse. She cried out in pain as she curled up in his arms.

"I've been worried about you," Jesse said as he started in the house. "I hope you didn't shoot this young lady instead of that cougar. She's barely breathing."

"No. Someone else did that. I found her laying out there with that gash on her head and the bullet in her shoulder." He threw the blankets back on the bed and watched the older man gingerly lay the woman down. "They just left her there to die."

"They? How many were there?"

"At least two the way I figure it. I followed their tracks quite a ways before I came across her. She must have been laying there for a couple of hours. Do you think we need Doctor Larson?"

Jesse lightly rubbed his finger over the shoulder wound. "Looks like the bullet passed through without hitting bone. If we keep the wound clean it ought to heal." Picking up a wet cloth he swabbed the gash on the woman's head and peered with a critical eye.

"This slash, on the other hand, looks troublesome. I got a feeling it may take more time. Let's see how she gets along tonight. Any idea who she is?"

"No, I've never seen her. There wasn't anything to identify her. If she had a horse it was long gone. It's like someone just dumped her there."

"Nobody goes up in those hills but thieves and riffraff looking for trouble. Do you think Reece would have any idea?"

"Well, I'd say Reece knows his share of thieves and riffraff but I can't say whether he'd know this girl," smiled Griff as he pulled up a chair by the bed.

Griffin sat next to the young woman as she lay sleeping. The oil lamp sitting on the bedside table offered little light in the room but he could see the quilt gently rising and falling, powered by her shallow breathing. He laid his hand on her forehead, already knowing it was warm. She was getting worse and he was at a loss for ways to keep her temperature down. His mind drifted as he remembered a time when he watched another woman fight for life, years before. His mother contracted pneumonia when he was younger and struggled for days, gasping for breath as her lungs filled with fluid. She lost that fight as he stood vigilantly with his family watching her slip away. He guarded his mother back then, just as he did this woman now and feared the worst. His father's grief, he recalled, was almost unbearable and as the heavy burden of those memories loomed over him, Griff was losing hope for this young woman's recovery.

He poured a pitcher of fresh water into a basin, soaking a cloth and wringing it out. Sitting beside the woman again, he wiped the beads of sweat from her face and arms then let the cool water dribble over her mouth to wet her dry lips.

"Is she any better?" asked Jesse in a low, whispered voice as he tiptoed in the room. He held out a cup of coffee and piece of hard bread and pulled up a stool from the end of the bed. "You've been sitting here for hours and there's no need to wear yourself down too."

"She's developing a fever," Griffin said. He tore off a chunk of bread and dunked it in the coffee. "She must have run for quite a while because she's completely worn down. She doesn't have much strength to fight."

"Do you think she knows the ones who hurt her?" Jesse asked.

"Hard to tell. She keeps repeating 'They're coming' like it's a warning. She must be reliving the whole ordeal in her mind. Makes you wonder why someone would try to kill her."

"She doesn't look like she could hurt a fly," said Jesse. "She could be running from the law, I guess. I better stop by the sheriff's office tomorrow. I'll ask if he wants me to take some men back up to the hills and pick up those tracks you saw. At least we would have an idea of which direction they headed. In the meantime, the best thing for her would be nourishment. She needs to eat something if she's going to survive that fever."

"She's not going to be eating for a while," said Griffin, pulling the blanket over the woman's shoulders. "I hope Doctor Larson has something for pain as well as infection. She'd rest more comfortably and maybe it would give her a break from whatever nightmare she's going through right now."

"I've seen gunshot wounds in men who were much stronger than this young girl," said Jesse. "I know you're struggling to find a way to keep her alive but to tell you the truth, I don't know that you can. She doesn't have much life left in her and hasn't been conscious since you brought her back." He gently placed his hand on Griff's back as he stood. "We've done everything we can and it does no good to fret. Eat something and then get some rest because she'll need you more if she wakes up. I'll be outside if you need me."

Griffin mustered a faint smile and took a sip of coffee. Jesse was a smart rancher with good instincts. He was Griff's ranch hand but more importantly, he was a friend. Jesse worked with Griff's father since they were young and new to the Nevada territory. Griffin and Jesse developed a close bond when Griff was a boy and in his opinion, there wasn't anything the older man couldn't do. When he set out on his own, Griff's father suggested Jesse go along to help. It was good advice. Together they had done well.

He leaned his chair back against the wall closing his eyes as he dozed off. Hours later he woke to the sound of screaming as he swung around blindly in the dark trying to find his gun. The woman sat up in bed, grabbing his arm and with a wild look in her eyes shouted, "You got no place to hide, girlie." She collapsed again in a fitful sleep.

Jesse burst through the door holding a shotgun and his own wild-eyed look. The bone chilling cry put them on edge and for a moment they stood there in silence, listening to the night as if expecting an explosion of man or beast to come crashing through the walls.

"That sounded like the cry of the Banshee," said Jesse, dropping his gun to his side as he stood watching the girl toss restlessly back and forth. "What do you suppose happened to her up in those hills?"

"I can't imagine, Jesse," said Griff, holding her hand gently. "But whoever did this should pay for her suffering."

"It's got me ready to jump out of my skin," said Jesse. "All this screaming and moaning gives me the willies." He sighed loudly and looked at Griff. “I think I’ll go out to the barn and check on the horses,”

“That’s probably a good idea. Make sure the back door is locked.”

Griff could hear the hinges on the barn door squeak as he sat back down. He knew there was nothing outside to be alarmed about and so did Jesse. Things were much too calm in the corral for any impending trouble. The circumstances involving this woman gave them both an uneasy feeling. He leaned his chair back against the wall and replayed the events of the day trying to extract every detail from his memory and closed his eyes once more.

CHAPTER 2

Forgotten Past

The smell of coffee filled the room as the woman drowsily opened her eyes. Her head throbbed as she scanned the room for something familiar. She laid in a bed centered against a long wall. To the left was a large window with curtains drawn, barely letting a crack of sunlight sneak through. A small nightstand next to the bed was covered with a white, crocheted doily and a large dresser stood against a wall to the right covered with a matching doily. She ran her fingers down the worn-out quilt tucked tightly around her and looked at the rocker in the corner, then back to a chair sitting beside the bed. Comfortable as this room might be, she had no idea where she was.

Sitting up, the young woman pushed the chair away from the bed, swinging her legs around until her feet touched the floor. Her nose crinkled into a face that was both shocked and disgusted when she realized she was wearing a man's white shirt dotted with blood stains. Worse yet, a man's grey flannel union suit cut off at the waist and held up by a rope covered the rest of her.

She gasped when she caught sight of her reflection in the full-length mirror. Her forehead was bandaged and face bruised. Her disheveled hair looked as if it had never been combed. She felt a dull aching in her back and reached to touch a bandaged area only to give out a yelp of pain. What have I done to myself, she thought?

The sound of voices in the next room caught her attention and she hoped someone there could explain what was going on. Taking a first step on the wood floor, the room began to spin. This was more difficult than expected. Gently moving across the room, she kept her balance by holding on to furniture until she reached the door and peered through.

Two men sat at a table, eating. They looked up as the young woman opened her mouth to speak but the dizziness and pain in her back made her weak and she grabbed for the wall as she slid down and dropped to the floor.

It was only a moment before she was scooped up and carried back to bed. She laid there with her eyes closed hoping the lightheadedness would subside. Someone was talking loudly in her ear and gently slapping her cheeks while another held her hand. She opened her eyes and squinted, then reached out to stop the man's hand before it met her face again.

"What on earth are you doing?" she said, trying to sit up. "My head is already killing me and slapping me senseless isn't going to help. Who are you?"

"I was just trying to bring you around," Griffin said with a grin, pleased to see the woman awake and sassy enough to kick up a fuss about a little pat on the face. "You gave us quite a scare when you dropped to the floor. You've been out for a while and caught us by surprise when we saw you standing in the kitchen."

"He's right," Jesse added still holding her hand. "You've had some rough nights and it's good to see you awake."

The woman looked puzzled as she studied the two men, not sure how to respond. She looked around the room once more with a dubious feeling. She was in a strange house with two men she'd never seen before and try as she may, had no recollection of how she got there. She recoiled with the realization she might be in danger.

"There's no reason to be scared, we're not going to hurt you," said Griff, reading her mind. "Like I said, we're trying to help. You were in bad shape when I found you. Your fever's been high and you haven't been in your right mind. Most nights you mumbled about things that made no sense. Jesse and I think you're lucky you recovered. Most people don't." He paused momentarily, embarrassed at his harsh explanation.

"Where am I?" the woman asked.

"The Emerald ranch. Or at least the west end of it. I'm Griffin Kelly, the owner. This is Jesse Anderson, my ranch hand."

"Ranch hand, horse trainer, steer wrangler and head cook most days," Jesse added with a warm smile and mischievous wink. "Lord knows what this ornery lad would do without me."

The young woman smiled back, studying their faces and looking for something familiar then surveyed her surroundings once more. "I still don't understand how I got here looking like this."

Jesse gave Griff a questioning look. "We were hoping you could fill us in on some of those questions. If you tell us where you come from we'll get in touch with your family. I bet they're worried after this long. Of course, the sheriff will need to talk to you."

"Why would the sheriff want to talk to me? Have I done something wrong?"

"You'll have to answer that yourself," said Jesse shooting a bewildered glance at Griff and thinking it was a suspicious way for this woman to act. A posse of men waited to scour half the countryside trying to solve the mystery of what happened to her. He wondered if she was as innocent as she pretended.

"We have no idea who you are, where you came from or even how you ended up in the hills half dead. I was the one who found you and brought you back here. We've spent nights nursing you through a fever and listening to your babbling about things neither of us understood and I don't think we're out of line to ask for an explanation. The sheriff is going to want some answers too. You might start with your name."

The woman wrestled with her thoughts, her eyes darting between the two men. She touched her bandaged head and then her shoulder as if to confirm her wounds, moaning in pain when she tried to sit up.

"I don't know."

"You don't know what?" said Griffin, perturbed with the way she was stalling.

"I don't know my name. I don't know the answers to any of those questions. I can't remember."

"See here young lady, this is not a game," said Jesse "Tell us who you are. If you've done something wrong it'll be up to the sheriff to decide what to do. Maybe it's best to turn you over to him now instead of waiting."

"Jesse please, threats aren't going to help." Griffin said. He gave the woman a skeptical frown. "You don't remember your own name?"

A look of fear crept over the woman's face, tears running down her cheeks as the sound of galloping horses and shouting voices pushed their way into her head. She closed her eyes, trembling. "Please don't hurt me," she suddenly cried out and for a moment the room was silent as the two men watched the girl shaking until Griff touched her hand to calm her.

"You have to believe me," she pleaded. "I can't remember."

Griffin studied the face of the frightened girl and his anger softened. It was a pretty face now that it was no longer covered with blood and dirt. Her brown eyes were begging for help and he couldn't believe this woman was deliberately trying to deceive them. She hadn't the hardened appearance of a saloon girl or women who followed outlaws. Her manner was delicate and the mumbling in her sleep when delirious made him feel she was telling the truth. He knew a person sometimes developed amnesia after a head injury and he had no reason to believe this wasn't the case with her.

"I'll believe you until I'm shown something different, but the sheriff is still going to want to speak to you. There's no avoiding that. He's going to want some answers."

"But I already told you, I don't have any for him," said the woman. "I have no idea who shot me or why? How can I possibly answer any questions?"

You don't know the sheriff," said Griff, smiling. "He's got a talent for finding information about people they didn't realize they had. Like all those nightmares you've been having. They must be full of clues and I guarantee it won't take Reece long to figure it out."

"What's to become of me after that?" asked the young woman. "You say I was shot but you haven't said by whom. What if they come back? Where am I to go? I have no home that I know of."

"You're going to stay here with me and Jesse for now. We've taken pretty good care of you so far and we'll be able to protect you." He looked at the older man with a wry smile. "Jesse, our self-proclaimed head cook, made some broth. We'll start with that. Try to eat something and don't worry about all this other business. It'll sort itself out. In the meantime, I'm going to ride in to town and let Doctor Larson and the sheriff know you're come to. I think it's best if Doc looks at your head. Jesse will watch over you until I get back. Now that you're awake, it won't be long until you remember."

CHAPTER 3

The Grace of God

Griffin slowly led the young woman into the front room where Jesse sat talking with another man. Their conversation stopped as she carefully sat down and waited for Griff to sit beside her. It was the first time she'd ventured out of the bedroom since she'd been there. After her fall in the kitchen, Griff and Jesse had confined her to bed, insisting she rest to regain her strength.

The main room was large with a stone fireplace covering one wall and leather furniture arranged around it. A painting hung above the mantel which, she supposed, was a picture of the ranch. The clock on the mantel ticked quietly as it kept time. She looked out the window at the front porch and saw the large barn with adjoining corral bordered by a grassy hill sloping down to the pasture. It was a peaceful sight.

Jesse smiled as he watched the young woman look meekly around, absorbing the surroundings. Her fear of the unknown had slowly subsided since the day Griffin brought her to the ranch and was replaced with a trust in the two men who nursed her back to health. He was proud of her determination to overcome her injuries and the uncertainty of her future.

"Another couple of days and you won't need help getting around at all. It's about time we let you out of that bedroom to see the rest of the ranch," he said. "I told Griff a day in the sunshine would bring color back to your cheeks faster than anything."

The woman blushed as she shyly glanced at Griff and then toward the man sitting quietly in a comfortable leather chair by the fireplace. She played with her hair nervously and fidgeted in her seat, not wanting to speak.

"I guess we need to introduce you to the sheriff," continued Jesse. "This is Reece Cameron."

The sheriff stood and lazily tipped his hat, nodding in the woman's direction. "Ma'am."

This man was certainly not what the woman expected. She imagined the sheriff to be older and maybe a little plumper, with grey hair. Reece Cameron was a tall, muscular man. His steel blue eyes seemed too serious for a man in his twenties and reflected the cautious nature of someone who carefully judged the people he met. He was strikingly handsome, and she blushed again at the thought of what he might think of her sitting there in baggy long johns and wrinkled white shirt she'd worn for days.

Of course, Griffin was handsome too. He was tall with brown hair that had a tousled look as if he just stepped inside from a windy day. She remembered his strong arms as he picked her up from the kitchen floor and carried her into the bedroom. His demeanor was different from the sheriff's. He possessed an endearing smile and a hint of mischief in his dark eyes with a touch of wit that put her at ease when he spoke. There was a kindness about him and a soft touch in those hands use to hard work.

"I was telling the sheriff that Doc Larson thinks it's definitely amnesia," said Jesse. "He said it's not uncommon for someone with a head injury like yours. Considering that business you went through up in the hills and being left for dead, it's not surprising you can't remember a thing. Doc said there's no telling when your memory will come back. Could be an hour, a day or even months."

"Jesse, for crying out loud," said Griffin shaking his head in frustration. "Can you come up with a kinder way to explain it. You're not making the situation any better for her."

"Don't be hard on him," said the woman, smiling at the older man. "Everything Jesse says is true and it's something I'm going to have to live with at least for now. She gazed out the window wishing this conversation was over. She knew the sheriff had come to question her about the day she was found and she still had no answers for him.

"The doc also said that being around familiar things will help," said Jesse, trying to make amends for his previous remarks. "That's why I think it'll do you good to get out some. You may find something you recognize if you can talk Griff into taking you for a ride today."

"I don't think I'm going to find anything familiar," the woman replied with a disheartened look. "Griff doesn't think I'm from around here and if no one recognizes me, I'm stuck with no knowledge of who I am."

'I don't think we've exhausted all possibilities yet," said the sheriff who was studying her face as she spoke. She gazed out the window as he continued to talk, wondering if he thought she was a criminal recently escaped from prison.

"We don't know for sure where you're from. People move in and out of this town all the time and there's nothing to say you don't have a family living close by."

"Has anyone asked about me?" said the woman. "If I live nearby why hasn't someone shown up looking for me? What if my memory never comes back? You have no idea how frightening it is to know nothing about yourself. I feel completely lost. I could pass someone on the street and never realize that I knew them. Griffin and Jesse have been so kind but I can't stay here forever. I don't know what I'll do." She looked out the window again, wondering how she would survive.

"Maybe you won't recognize people but I was hoping someone might recognize you," replied the sheriff. He glanced at Griff who shook his head disapprovingly.

"It seems the sheriff and I disagree on how to handle this investigation."

"Investigation? Am I being investigated?" The woman looked disappointedly at Griff. "So, you think I've done something wrong?"

"We don't think you've done anything, but Reece is trying to figure out who these people are and that takes some scrutiny."

"These men are dangerous, no matter who they are," said Reece, leaning forward in his chair and resting his arms loosely on his legs. "We don't know what your involvement is and why they were intent on harming you. Based on what they did, I suspect they're a mean bunch and I'd like to find them before they try to kill someone else."

I'm afraid we don't have much to go on. I rode east through the hills with a couple of men, including Jesse. We picked up their tracks heading north. Looks like they doubled back toward Reno but it's difficult to track in those hills and I'm afraid we lost the trail. I don't suppose anything about Reno would be familiar to you?"

"Nothing sounds familiar to me right now, sheriff," answered Grace with a nervous laugh. "That's the whole problem. I'm unable to help with any details. I don't know that I've ever been to Reno. Is that where you think these men are from?"

"Right now, I'm just grasping for any clues I can find. I don't think we need to tell you that your memory is our best hope for discovering what happened. I sent a message to the marshal in Carson City but haven't heard a thing back. If somebody shows up that doesn't belong in those parts, he'll let us know. I've also sent messages to a couple of towns in the area to see if they are missing anyone matching your description. I'm afraid I haven't heard back on that either."

"Why don't you and Griffin agree on the investigation?" the woman asked.

The sheriff again glanced at Griff who hesitated before speaking. "None of us think it was an accident you encountered those men and it stands to reason they think you're dead. In my opinion, it's best to keep them thinking that. It'll buy Reece some time and keep you safer if you stay here on the ranch and out of the public's eye."

"I agree with that," said the sheriff. "But with no leads and no identity we're stuck. That's why I was hoping to take you to town. If someone recognizes you it'll be a lot easier to solve this mystery. Griff is a little jumpy about letting you out of his sight for now."

"But I want to go to town," said the woman. "I want to solve this mystery more than anything. I don't care who these people are or why they hurt me or even if I'm involved in something bad. Anything is better than not knowing."

"I still think it's dangerous," said Griffin.

"Please," said the woman looking at Griff with mournful eyes. "I may have family looking for me and this might be the only way to find them. It's worth the risk to me."

Griff hated the idea of taking the young woman to town and resented the sheriff for bringing up the idea. She was right in thinking she could walk down the street and not recognize the very person that put a bullet in her shoulder. How could he possibly defend her against a situation like that? The woman reached out, lightly touching his hand and smiled. He returned her smile then glared at the sheriff.

"Alright, but we're not staying long. We can stop at Miller's then we're coming right back. I don't want to wear you down on your first day out."

Smiling broadly, the woman squealed softly and gave Griff an awkward hug before cringing as a sharp pain stabbed her shoulder. She quickly looked away, afraid Griff might change his mind and caught the sheriff's eye as he smiled and winked.

"I'll hitch up the wagon," said Jesse. "You might as well stop at the seed and supply while you're in town. No use wasting a trip."

The sheriff rose to leave and tipped his hat once more. "Have a nice time in town, ma'am. You let me know if these two don't treat you right. In the meantime, you might want to come up with a name. Folks might find it unusual for Griff to be stammering over what to call you."

"Reece has a point," said Griffin. "It feels odd not to be able to use a name."

"It feels odd not to have one," the young woman replied.

Then I guess we need to pick one out," Griffin said. "What would you like to be called?"

"I haven't really thought about it." She sat with a puzzled look, deep in thought. "I'm afraid I haven't a single idea."

"There are countless possibilities," said Griff. "How about Rascal? That's my horse's name."

The young woman laughed. "Would you want to be called Rascal?"

"I believe that name has been used in connection with Griff more than once," said Reece, chuckling. "Along with a few others we don't want to mention. Leave it to him to want to name a woman after his horse. He can't be trusted with this process."

"You got any ideas, Reece? You seem full of opinions today," said Griff

"She needs a pretty name to go along with her pretty smile," said the sheriff grinning as he pondered the idea. "Something fitting."

The young woman stood shyly as both men contemplated her features and how to decide on a name for this frail girl they didn't know. It would only be a temporary moniker of course, but neither wanted to offend her by the suggestion of something unbecoming. They looked at each other and back to the woman until finally a smile crept over Griff's face. "Judging by the shape you were in when I found you, I'd say you're alive only by the grace of God. I think we'll call you Grace."

"It's perfect," said Reece. "Although I hate to admit Griff was the one who came up with it."

"It's a beautiful name," said the young lady as she curtsied to the two men. "Pleased to meet you Mr. Kelly and an honor to know you sheriff. My name is Grace. I can't tell you how much I appreciate what you're doing for me. I don't know how I'm going to repay you."

"The honor is mine," said Griff with a bow. "You can call me Griffin or Griff or even Rascal. All three fit, but Mr. Kelly is reserved for my father, especially around these parts."

"Now that we have this name thing settled, I'm heading back," said the sheriff, starting for the door. "I'm afraid you're stuck with Jesse and Griff for now, Grace. I hope it won't be too painful for you."

"She couldn't get any luckier, Reece" Griff replied. He looked at the young woman with a wry smile. " Now run along sheriff and chase some criminals while I take this young lady to town."

"Right," Reece said sarcastically over his shoulder as he walked toward the door. "Careful you don't get lost."

"You're going to need something to wear besides that," said Jesse as he entered from the other room carrying a folded dress and looking at Grace's drooping pants which hung around her hips, in danger of falling off and dropping to the floor.

"We weren't sure of the size," added Griff, rather embarrassed at their offering. "It belongs to my sister but I'm afraid it's going to have to do for now. Miller Mercantile will have something to fit. We can go anytime you're ready."

Looking flustered, the young woman pulled the pants up and tried to tighten the belt. "Thank you. I must look a fright. I'd love to take a bath first," she said brushing her hair back from her face. "I can barely stand myself. I can't imagine what the sheriff must have thought."

"He thought the same thing as the rest of us. You're recovering from a serious wound and haven't been in any condition to worry about what your hair looks like," said Griff then corrected himself, stumbling through an apology, looking at the older man for help. "Not that you look bad. I mean, you look good, doesn't she Jesse?"

The woman chuckled and looked around. "It's alright. I understood what you meant. Is there somewhere I could clean up?"

"There's a small room off the kitchen with a tub. Nothing fancy, of course, but it's the best we have. I'll get some hot water. You'll find soap and a couple of towels in a cabinet. I'll be waiting outside."

An hour later the woman stepped out on the porch looking like a different person. The borrowed dress was big and the boots she wore the day she was found were scuffed and covered with drops of blood, but her long brown hair glistened as it caught the gleaming sun and Griff smiled when he saw her standing by the door. Jesse was right, he thought. A day outside would bring out the color in her cheeks. He was amazed at the transformation. This girl had a charm hidden under that dirt and for the first time, she seemed happy.

"You look nice, Grace," he said, grinning as he helped her in the wagon and snapped the reins, heading past the barn and through the gate of the split rail fence marking the entrance to the ranch.

"I smell better too, which is a good thing since you're taking me to town. I wouldn't want to embarrass you. Thank goodness you have a sister. I can't imagine what I would have worn without her," said the woman. She took a deep breath and looked around. "This is a beautiful ranch. Such a peaceful view. You must do well raising cattle with these pastures. Plenty of water and enough grazing room to keep quite a herd well fed. Does all of the Emerald look like this?"

"Most of it," Griff laughed. "You seem to know something about ranching. That might be the first clue about your background. Could be you were raised in the cattle business."

"It seemed like a natural thing to say," Grace said, surprising herself.

"How about you, Griffin? What made you decide to become a rancher?"

"It's in my blood," said Griff. "My father is a rancher. He owns the Emerald ranch. Some of the best timber and pasture land around."

"I thought you owned the Emerald."

"I do. This part of it at least. I know it sounds confusing. This was all owned by my father originally. I lived with him and my two brothers and sister until a couple of years ago when my brother Matt got married and my father gave him his share of the Emerald. Matt and his wife, Elizabeth, renamed their ranch the Circle K. I decided it was a good time to take my share too."

"To start your own family?"

"Well, not yet but some day, maybe. We had no choice but to learn the cattle business. Matt is the oldest and has a knack for always doing the right things to please my father. He's a good rancher and the one Pa relied on the most.

Rachel, my sister looks so much like my mother who died years ago, I believe it haunts my father and he pampers her horribly. We all do I guess. Being the only girl, I think it was hardest on her after Ma died. I admit Rachel makes an effort to take her place in running the household and keep us all happy which isn't an easy feat sometimes. I don't think I realized that until I built my own place. My sister has a mind of her own, just like my pa and he would be lost without her. She's got a big heart and a compassionate soul.

My younger brother, Lance," Griffin said, shaking his head and laughing. "No one knows what he's doing half the time. He was small when our mother died. My father was so grief stricken, there were times when he didn't notice us. Not a good thing for any of us, when we were growing up. I think we were all lost for a time. Matt got through by helping my father. Not like he had a choice. I was usually stuck watching Rachel. She tagged behind me and my friend where ever we went, much to our chagrin. Lance spent a large portion of that period with our family friends, the Spencers. They lost their only child and Lance filled that void for them. Especially Margaret. She and my mother were close and I believe it was her wish that the Spencers become my brother's guardian angels. I don't think Lance cares too much for ranch life and likes to visit my mother's family back east. I wouldn't be surprised if he ends up moving back there someday."

"Why did you decide to take your share of the land? Doesn't your father need your help on his ranch now that Matt is married?"

"Well...Pa and I don't always see eye to eye. I tried to follow in Matt's footsteps but I'm a different person. My father doesn't take me serious most of the time so we're usually at odds with each other. When Matt left, I figured it was time for me to go too. It gave me a chance to be on my own. I'm an Emerald man at heart and now I have my own slice of it. Most people around know the difference."

"Where does Jesse fit into all of this?" asked Grace. "I've watched you two and you seem as close as a father and son would be."

"Jesse worked on my pa's ranch for as long as I can remember and I guess he's like a father to me. He'd never think of interfering when my pa and I argued but he was always there to take me fishing for the afternoon until Pa and I got past our differences. I was relieved when he asked to come help me get my ranch started. I don't know what I'd do without him or that I could ever repay him for all his hard work."

"I don't know that he expects any payment. I get the feeling his is as happy to be on the ranch as you are to have him."

Maybe so." Griff gave Grace a little nudge. "Just don't complement him on his cooking. It'll go to his head." He snapped the reins to quicken the step of the horses. "We'll be in town soon."

⅄

Miller Mercantile was the largest of three general stores in town and one of the oldest. Juanita Miller worked alongside her husband to build their business in the early days when the silver mines flourished. It was a towering two-story structure which sat on a corner of Main street, the most prominent location to be had.

Juanita was an organized woman who kept the store well stocked with merchandise neatly displayed. Lady's clothing was strategically separated from general household goods to give women a private place to shop, away from nervous husbands concerned about their bill when Juanita's charms made ladies' fashion seem irresistible. She prided herself on having the best selection of clothing available in the state. Her reputation was important and she made sure everyone who would listen knew that women traveled from as far as Carson City to buy clothing at her store. Juanita was a heavy woman in her fifties with a large bust and graying hair she kept tightly wrapped in a bun high on her head. Despite her aging figure, she was well dressed and never a hair out of place.

Mr. Miller was a timid man who knew his wife had the better mind for business and was content to handle day to day operations and count the money stacked in their register at the end of each day.

"Is this the young lady who was injured?" asked Juanita with a critical eye as Griff approached while Grace looked around. "What a lovely face. Goodness, look at that poor girl. So much bruising. I'd like to get my hands on the person who did this. I hope Reece finds him soon."

"He's working on it, Mrs. Miller," said Griffin with a placating smile. "We were hoping to keep this whole thing quiet until Reece had time to track the culprits down. We think she'll be safer that way."

"Well I'm afraid it's too late for that. I believe most of the town has already heard the story. You know you can't keep a thing like that a secret for too long. What's she wearing?"

"It's one of Rachel's old dresses. The best I could do under the circumstances. That's why we've come to you. She's going to need some clothes and if you can keep my sister happy then Grace should be easy. She needs everything. Shoes, dresses, maybe a hat and all those things you women wear underneath."

Mrs. Miller gave Griff a curious smile, answering in a whispered voice. "You let me take care of her, Griffin. I've got some lovely things that will be perfect. My, but she is thin. I don't see how you're ever going to fatten her up with Jesse's cooking. Let me speak to the garden club about taking some food to the ranch."

"We're doing just fine, Mrs. Miller. Grace isn't much for company right now and again, we're trying to keep things low-keyed. She's getting stronger every day so please tell the garden club that we send our thanks but Jesse's cooking is plenty. Now about her clothes."

"Well of course, I have a few things that will fit but you might have to bring her back for alterations. Why don't you go on down to the Elkhorn and find the sheriff? I'll send word when we're done. It shouldn't take too long. Now, young lady," she called as she turned toward Grace, estimating her size "I have a brown print that will match your eyes perfectly."

⅄

The cowboy stood partially hidden behind his horse as he tied the reins around the post and watched the buckboard come to a halt in front of Miller Mercantile. A menacing smile spread slowly across his unshaved face when he recognized the young woman as she was helped from the wagon and escorted into the store. He had spent the morning at the Elkhorn Saloon looking for information about a woman killed in the hills. His anger smoldered when he learned the girl wasn't dead after all, despite what he had been told. She was, instead, alive and recovering on a ranch owned by Griffin Kelly while the sheriff searched for a group of cattle rustlers suspected of being involved. This posed a problem for the cowboy because the young woman could identify him and the others and he wouldn't let that happen. She was a problem that he would have to take care of himself this time. He chuckled as he thought of his good luck in spotting this woman when he was about to leave. Glaring at the store front, he deliberated over his next move and watched as the man who escorted the woman to town appeared at the door and walked down the street toward the Elkhorn, leaving the woman unguarded inside the store. The cowboy spit on the ground and scowled, waiting until the man entered the saloon. He looked around for others passing by, then walked across the street and peered into the large front window of Miller Mercantile.

Juanita Miller turned Grace around, pinching the waist of her dress and releasing it again. She mumbled to herself as she knelt and measured the distance from the bottom of the hem to the floor. It was awkward for Grace at first to have Juanita spin her in all directions, measuring her waist and hips, constantly humming as she threw a dress over Grace's head then proceeded to tighten the bodice or check a sleeve length only to declare it unsuitable and pick up another.

"I think you're ready, my dear. You should have enough things to wear for now. Griffin will need to bring you back on another day. I know he's anxious about staying too long. I've done what I can in this short amount of time but I believe he'll be satisfied. I hope you're pleased too."

"It's all wonderful, Mrs. Miller," Grace replied, looking at her reflection in the mirror. "I'm very pleased. Do you think it would be alright to get a ribbon to match this dress?"

"Pick out a couple," Juanita called.

Grace walked to the front of the store and began to sort through the spools of colored ribbon. Finding one she liked, she picked it up and held the end, pulling out a section about a foot long. It was a pretty color when the natural light shined on it and would look fine with the brown dress. Smiling as she thought of Griff's reaction when he saw her new things, something outside caught her eye and looking through the window she saw the grim stare of the bearded cowboy. It was a face she'd seen before. Panic overwhelmed her as his hardened eyes fixed on hers. Memories of the sound of approaching horses pounded in her head and her knees grew weak. Her hand gently pressed against her bruised forehead as she closed her eyes to shut out the sight of the threatening figure staring through the window and mumbled, "They're coming." Dropping the ribbon to the floor, she let out a scream and fainted.

CHAPTER 4

The Shed Door

"May I help?" asked Grace when she entered the kitchen, startling Griffin. She closed her eyes and took a deep breath, sniffing the air. "It smells good. I thought Jesse was head cook?"

"Jesse just thinks he's head cook. I'm the real chef. You're up early. I thought you'd be exhausted after yesterday's ordeal. You had a pretty sleepless night."

By the time Griff and Reece made it to Miller's, Juanita had revived Grace and the cowboy in the window was nowhere to be found. The sheriff checked the nearby alley and scoured streets, but there was no sign of the mysterious man who frightened her.

She gave them a description although it would match a dozen men in town. "Medium height, beard, dirty blonde hair, wearing an even dirtier green shirt. "He had hatred in his eyes," murmured Grace. "I remember the hatred the most."

Despite recognizing his face, she remembered nothing more about him or his connection to her past, although the logical conclusion was that he was among those who hurt her. Reece questioned men at the Elkhorn who recalled seeing a cowboy matching Grace's description but they could offer few details. The sheriff set out with a group of men in the direction of the hills hoping to pick up a trail or find a clue to his identity but no one had heard back from Reece yet.

Griffin was angry at the sheriff for talking him into taking Grace away from the safety of the ranch and into town. He was angrier with himself for leaving her alone at Miller's. When they returned home, she went immediately to bed, taking the headache medicine Doctor Larson left. Griff tried to get her to eat supper later in the evening but she would have none of it. He was afraid the experience in town might set back her recovery at a time when she was starting to regain confidence.

Sleep did not come easy for either of them. Griff could hear Grace muttering in her sleep and knew she was tormented by her recurring dreams. She cried out to him in the night and when he entered her room he found her huddled in the corner, certain she heard scratching at the window and whispered voices coming from beyond the trees. Jesse was sent in search of the source but could find no sign of anyone. Her fears were dismissed as part of the nightmare and Griff wondered if she would ever be able to live a normal life again. Now, she was standing in the kitchen acting as if nothing happened.

"I admit it was a rough night," Grace answered, embarrassed when she thought of cowering in the corner. She knew they didn't believe her story of the voices but she was convinced she heard the muffled sounds near the window. The face of the bearded cowboy was still on her mind. Whoever he was, she was sure he had come for her.

"I'd like to help if you'd let me," she said peering over Griff's shoulder as he stood at the stove pushing strips of bacon around in the cast iron skillet.

"I guess you can start the biscuits while I finish up," Griffin said. "The bacon is almost ready. My father bought this old stove for my mother when he built their house. He's never been able to part with it, so he gave it to me when I moved here. It's a little beat up but it still does the job."

"Your father must be a kind man even though you two butt heads at times. It fact your entire family sounds wonderful and so supportive."

"He's been good to all of us. Pa and my brothers built this house with me, just like we helped build Matt's. It's the same with most families around here. My sister picked out the drapes and furniture. She likes to do that sort of thing. She was even willing to part with my mother's doilies. They're in the bedroom. Ma made that old quilt on the bed when I was small. Kind of keeps her memory alive I guess. I am, indeed, a lucky man and forget that sometimes."

Grace was envious. A father who shares his success and siblings willing to contribute their time to help one another was such a gift. Was her family as close, she wondered? If so, where were they? Looking for her and worried for her safety? Griff and Jesse went out of their way to make her feel comfortable but she was homesick just the same, even if she didn't know where home was.

She touched the hard edge of the stove and a vision appeared in her mind. She saw a warm room where sunbeams danced on the floor and the smell of morning breakfast lingered. Wrapping her hand tightly around the handle of the heavy skillet, she smiled. Besides the menacing face of a cowboy peering through Miller's front window, this fleeting image was the first returning memory she'd had. Grace closed her eyes, trying to enhance the moment.

"I've cooked on a stove like this," she suddenly declared.

"You have?" Griffin said as he watched her staring at the skillet. "What do you remember?"

"Well basically just the stove," she giggled, a little embarrassed at the outburst. "They're temperamental if you don't have the fire just right." She opened the door and adjusted the logs with a poker.

"If the fire is too high the biscuits won't cook evenly. Nobody likes a biscuit burned on the outside and still doughy in the middle." She closed the door and turned to look at Griffin. "That should do it."

"If you remember the stove, do you remember a kitchen to go with it?"

"Not really. It's more like a puzzle with familiar pieces that don't seem to be in the right place. I can't get the picture exactly the way it should be as if someone or something important is missing. Rooms, smells, voices, all appear in my head although none are recognizable. There is one voice that stands out. One that is soft spoken and comforting. It's like a whisper in my ear offering assurances of hope. I feel as if I'm on the verge of remembering if I could put all these pieces together."

"You got that coffee ready," grunted Jesse as he entered the room. He walked to the stove and shook the metal coffee pot then carried it to the table, placing it on a trivet.

"Grace is remembering," said Griff, glancing her way. "She may be heading home sooner than we thought."

"Not before I get my coffee, I hope," said Jesse. "I'm going to need my breakfast before sending her off. What's come back to you Grace? I knew it wouldn't be long."

"The stove," she answered. "I know it's not much but it's a start. I could remember everything by the time the sheriff gets back and can help solve this whole case. I'm sure he'd be relieved to have it finished." She gave Jesse a hug and laughed. "I promise I'll let you eat before I leave."

"I'm real happy to hear that, although I don't think Reece is going to give up too easily," said Jesse. "Griff and I have some things to do in the lower end of the pasture today if you're feeling up to staying here in the house alone, Grace."

"Will you be alright by yourself?" Griff said hesitantly. "We'll both be within shouting distance if you need us. There's been a few things I've neglected lately that need my attention."

Grace was anxious although she didn't want to let Griff and Jesse know it. She couldn't ignore the incident in town yesterday and the voices last night were real to her even if no one else believed they existed. Still, she understood Jesse and Griff had their own work and their own responsibilities.

"If it really bothers you, one of us can stay here in the house," Griffin said, noticing the strain on her face. "I know this has been difficult for you."

"No, I can't let you neglect the ranch. I'll be fine. From the looks of this kitchen, it could use a good scrubbing. I'm sure the rest of the house could stand to be cleaned also. That will keep me busy most of the day. I remember how to use the stove so I'll have supper ready when you get back. I really want to do my part as long as I'm here."

Griffin was relieved. The last couple of weeks had been demanding for all of them. He felt guilty about wanting some time away but he hadn't slept since he brought Grace home. Her restless nights were his restless nights and the scare they had in town the day before, left him tense. He wanted time away to work the ranch and relieve the pressure. He looked forward to losing himself in a hard day of work followed by a peaceful night's sleep. He also wanted time to think about what to do next. It's was true that Grace was remembering but Reece hadn't any luck tracking down the men who tried to kill her and wasn't any closer to finding out why someone wanted her dead. After the encounter with the cowboy in town, Griff wasn't convinced that Grace was out of danger.

"There's a bunch of books in the store room," Griff said. "If you want something to pass the time."

"Yeah, if you feel like scraping the dust off them," said Jesse. "I doubt they've been touched since we hauled them over from his pa's ranch when Griff moved."

"Store room?" Grace said, looking at Griff in confusion. "Why haven't I noticed a store room before?"

"It's in the back of the house. I keep the door closed most of the time," answered Griffin.

"You've been a little preoccupied, Gracie," Jesse said. "About the only thing in there is those books and that old bed he's been sleeping on."

"You've been sleeping on an old bed in a storeroom?" said Grace, flustered. "I had no idea. After what you've done for me and now to find you've sacrificed your own bedroom. I feel ashamed I never thought to ask about your sleeping arrangements. I suppose you're sleeping on the roof," she said turning to Jesse.

"No, ma'am. It's not come to that yet. I have a room built especially for me off the barn that suits me just fine. For years I slept in a bunkhouse with a bunch of wild cowboys. Half of them snoring or talking in their sleep and the other half playing cards all night. It feels great to finally have a room all to myself."

"I'll move my things out of your room immediately. If anyone sleeps in the storeroom it should be me."

"No one is moving anywhere. It's not as bad as Jesse says and I sleep there whenever Rachel visits. If my own sister kicks me out of my room, you shouldn't feel bad."

"Well then, the least I can do is make sure it's clean. You and Jesse don't have to worry about a thing," said Grace as she rose from her chair and peeped down the hall toward the closed door of the store room.

Once she was left alone, Grace enjoyed the morning. She realized, while washing dishes, that she hadn't had any time alone since coming to the ranch. She was revitalized and danced around the house. Having a job to do gave her a sense of independence...a sense of control over her own life and she forgot about the unpleasant events from the day before.

Once most of the cleaning was finished, she peeked in the store room at the back of the house. It was much smaller than the large bedroom she was sleeping in. Pulling back the curtains revealed dust and disorder with cluttered furniture and unopened boxes. The unmade bed looked to be something primitive from older times. It was made of logs hewn from an Aspen tree and held together with nails and leather straps. The frame jiggled when she touched it and she paused for a moment thinking it might fall into a million pieces before her eyes. That can't be comfortable, she thought as she touched the mattress stuffed with goose down. It had seen better days and made her feel even more guilty about taking Griff's room.

There was a small wooden desk against one wall. Perched atop was an oil lamp, its glass chimney blackened with soot. Grace removed the chimney, wiped it clean and placed it back on the lamp, checking first to see if the oil supply was sufficient. A Barrister bookcase was pushed against the other wall. She crouched in front of the shelves and ran her fingers along the bindings of the books, skimming the titles as she went. A gun rack mounted on the wall housed several rifles.

Clothes were thrown on the end of the bed and tossed over a chair. Grace shook her head as she grabbed sheets and clothing, throwing them into a pile. She sighed deeply and glanced toward the books then turned around and picked up the mound of dirty shirts and linens and headed for the door. Her time, she decided, would be better spent doing laundry. She would leave reading for another day.

Having cleaned the shirts belonging to Jesse and Griff and having been shocked at how dirty a man's clothes could become, Grace dragged the laundry basket through the back door and into the warm sunshine. What a beautiful day, she thought. No wonder Griffin and Jesse wanted to work outside.

She stood for a moment on the little porch looking at the back yard. There was an old tool shed about thirty feet from the house. The clothes line, which was strung from the shed to the house, sagged in the middle. Griffin has indeed been neglecting things, she thought. The grass was several feet high around the shed and she struggled to make a path while carrying the heavy laundry. She set the basket down and stared at the clothes line trying to decide if the rope should be tightened when she heard a rustling behind her.

She turned to look but saw nothing. A breeze was causing the high grass to wave and leaves to rustle on their limbs, but no sign of animals. The cattle were grazing in the distance and Grace wondered if Griff was close to finishing his work.

Turning back to the line, she picked up a shirt and started to hang it. Again, her attention was turned, as a covey of quail rose loudly from its nest as if flushed out by an intruder. "Could be a feral cat," she said to herself uneasily as she finished hanging the clothes.

She picked up the basket and made her way toward the house when she was startled by the sound of the shed door bumping against its frame. Dropping the basket, she ran to the house and slammed the door behind her. She was shaking as she leaned against the wooden frame. The knob pressed against her back as she stood, intently listening for sounds. Thoughts of last night and the voices outside her window came back and for a moment she was frozen where she stood.

She gasped in fear as the knob on the front door began to rattle. Someone was trying to get in. She could hear footsteps on the porch and wondered where Griff and Jesse were now and if they could really hear her screams. The rifles in the gun rack hanging on the wall in the spare room came to mind and Grace began to move quietly in that direction. Sneaking on tip toes, she slipped back into the store room and grabbed a gun, checked to see if it was loaded, then headed toward the front door and the rattling doorknob.

Standing by the side of the window, Grace peered through the curtains. She saw no one. The footsteps were silent and the doorknob no longer made noise as she looked as far as she could see on either side of the porch and out to the barn. She breathed a sigh of relief and relaxed momentarily, ready to pass the whole experience off as her active imagination when the rattling began again, only this time at the back door. She held her breath trying to remember if it was locked, then heard the door open and someone walk inside.

It made no difference if Griff was close enough to hear or not because when she opened her mouth, not a sound came out. She raised the gun and stood poised for whatever may come next, listening to footsteps and the soft ticking from the clock on the mantle

CHAPTER 5

DEAR JOHN

"Grace, are you home?" A voice called out from the kitchen. "It's Sheriff Cameron."

Grace lowered the gun, exhaling loudly as tears ran down her cheeks. She dropped to her knees in a heap of sobs unable to gather the strength to stand again. Reece helped her up and held her in his arms as she cried.

"I didn't mean to scare you. I saw Griff down by the road and he said you were doing a little reading this afternoon. He told me to come on up and wait for him. I knocked but no one answered. I tried the door and it was locked. You must have been out back. I was worried when I couldn't find you."

"I'm so sorry, Sheriff," Grace said as she pulled a hankie from her pocket and blew her nose. "You're right, I was out back hanging up the laundry and had such an eerie feeling that someone was watching. I admit, I didn't see a thing. Just some quail and movement in the grass but it didn't feel right. When I heard the shed door banging, I was scared. I guess I'm jittery"

"You have a right to be on edge," Reece said, not letting go of Grace. "It's not a good thing for you to be left alone so soon."

"I didn't know it was going to be a problem. I can't stay locked up in a room ready to shoot everyone that shows up at the door. I need to go on with my life. I doubt those men will ever be caught so I have to learn to live with that."

"What's going on here and who do you plan to shoot?" Griffin stood leaning against the front door with his arms folded glaring at Reece as his eyes moved down to where the Sheriff's arms were still tightly around Grace. "It appears I've missed something."

"Griff, I thought someone was watching me," Grace said as she crossed the room to where he stood, tears still running down her cheeks. "When I was hanging clothes in the back of the house." She relayed her story to both men and how the sheriff found her holding a gun when he walked in to the front room.

"Why didn't you call out for me? I told you Jesse and I would both be here in a minute if we thought there was the slightest chance you were in trouble. Jesse's been in the barn working most of the day."

"It all happened so fast I didn't have time to think. I just dropped the laundry basket and ran back to the house."

"Grace," Reece asked. "Was the shed door open when you went out to hang up the clothes?" He shot a dubious look at Griff.

"I don't recall, but Griff, I want you to lock it before night. It makes my hair stand on end every time I hear it banging."

Griff glanced at the sheriff again, frowning as he shook his head ever so slightly. Some of the details of Grace's story weren't right and he sensed Reece was thinking the same thing. "We'll look at it later. Don't let it bother you anymore."

"There's a reason why I stopped by today," said Reece, pulling a saddle bag off his shoulder and gently laying it on the table. "I've been up north since yesterday scouring every inch of those hills. We ran into a miner who claims he found a black filly, still saddled, grazing along a stream about two days ago, not more than five miles from where Griff found you. It was obvious the horse had been ridden hard. No rider was around so the old man took the filly to Carson City and sold her along with the saddle. He kept this bag though."

Grace looked at the saddle bag lying on the table. It was made of fine cowhide leather and ornately stitched. The initials A. B. encircled by a border of roses were etched in the middle. She sat motionless, suspecting it belonged to her.

"Do you think this is mine?"

I was hoping," answered the sheriff. "It would provide some needed clues. He opened the bag and pulled out a piece of paper neatly folded in half and then half again, handing it to Grace. "There's not much in there but this. You should read it."

Grace opened the paper and silently read the letter.

My Darling,

I think we've both known for some time that the love we share was not the kind that would last forever. I will only make you miserable if we continue with our plans to marry. I am leaving today for Denver where I hope to establish my own business. I am grateful to your father. I release you from our commitment and wish you much happiness.

With love,

John

Folding the paper again, she held it in her hands, crinkling it slightly while staring at the carved letters on the saddle bags. "Well," she finally said with a forced smile. "It appears I've been jilted...by a man named John."

The two men looked on in silence until Reece shot a pleading look toward Griff, urging him to respond.

"It's his loss," said Griff, blurting out the words, nervously. He ran his fingers through his hair, looking flustered. He looked at Reece for support, nodding toward Grace.

"Yeah, it's his loss," repeated Reece. "I mean, it's probably best for everyone. Right, Griff?"

"That's right," Griff repeated confidently. "No gentleman would do this to a lady, especially one like you. Don't you pay any mind to that letter. Why any man would be..."

"I have a father," Grace finally said light-heartedly after a moment of listening to the two men grasp awkwardly for condolences. "This is very good news. I have family and a horse. At least I did before it was sold. Most importantly, I have initials. Any guess about what they stand for?"

"I think we could rule out Grace," smiled Griff. There must be a dozen names that start with the letter A.

"Maybe they're the horse's initials," she laughed, opening the flap. "I guess you'll have to continue to call me Grace for a while longer. I might like that better than my own."

She stuck her hand in the bag and pulled out a beaded, silk purse. Even though it had been stored in leather, it held the scent of flowers and she took a moment to enjoy the aroma.

"Lavender," she exclaimed. "It's my favorite and a welcome change considering there isn't much in the way of gentle, feminine scents around this house. I suppose that's to be expected since it's been occupied by men until recently."

"Hey, Jesse and I smell good." Griff grinned as he took a whiff of his under arms, then shrugged his shoulders. "Well, most of the time we do." He looked at Reece who shook his head and grunted.

Grace opened the clasp and peered inside. "Empty. I guess the miner took the money. Oh well, finders, keepers." She shrugged her shoulders and smiled as she passed it to Griffin.

"A little thing like that wouldn't hold much," said Reece. "My guess is that it didn't contain a lot for the miner to spend in the first place."

"It looks fancy," said Griff, inspecting the beaded bag. He opened the gold clasp and ran his fingers around the inside as if hoping to come up with a hidden coin. "Like something my sister would own. What else is in there?"

These crackers," she answered, pulling out the hard squares and scraping off flecks of dirt. "Yuk, how old is this stuff? This had to belong to the miner because I can't imagine why I would want to eat something like this, unless it was meant for the horse."

"Hardtack. Jesse says they use to carry it in the war. Soldiers would dunk it in their coffee to soften it up. Sometimes it was the only thing they had to eat on a long campaign. It'll last forever."

"Looks like it's been around since the beginning of time. I'd have to be desperate." Grace, shivered at the thought of having the hard, bland crackers as a meal."

"You'd be glad to have it if you were hungry enough and planning to hide out for a couple of days," said Reece. "Which is a possibility in your case. We have no idea where you were headed or how long you'd been running from those men."

Grace reached in again and found a bandana wadded up, she supposed, by the miner. Picking it up by her finger tips she sniffed the tattered red material, repulsed by the thought of what it might have been used for.

"This is something I could have done without seeing," she said, setting it aside.

"It's gonna take some strong lye soap to get that clean," said Griff with a smirk.

"I think it might be best to burn it," answered Grace, cringing.

Once again, she dug her hand into the bag. Lying on the bottom, hidden by the dirty bandana was a leather tobacco pouch tightly secured with strings and she slowly opened it with dread, hating to think of what she might discover inside.

Her hands folded around an oval object wrapped in a small white piece of linen. Carefully pealing the edges of the fabric, she uncovered a miniature, painted portrait of a young woman who appeared to be about twenty years old. She smiled affectionately, knowing this woman must be dear to her.

"It's you," Griff said softly.

"Me? Why do you say that? Look at her dress and hair. This was painted too long ago to be me."

"Maybe so but you both have the same eyes and chin. You must be related. Perhaps she's your mother."

Grace studied the picture again. The dark eyes were the same and round chin looked similar. "Do you think so?"

"I do indeed," he said, smiling. "She's too old to be a sister so she must be your mother. You both have the same delicate beauty."

Grace blushed at his words and held tight to the portrait, wondering where this woman was now and if she would ever meet her.

"Griff's right," said Reece. "You and the woman in that picture do look alike. That should be proof, this saddle bag belongs to you. "She's a pretty woman, whoever she is."

Grace smiled and gently wrapped the picture in the linen, setting it aside. Feeling around in the bag for anything else she might have missed, she found a bulge on the back side of the flap under a fabric lining.

"This is odd," she said, running her fingers over the bump. "Saddle bags usually don't have a lining, do they?"

Griff reached in his pocket and pulled out a knife. He made a small slit at the edge of the fabric and stuck his fingers into the opening, touching two objects resting on the bottom. "There's something in here, alright." He turned the flap upside down allowing a comb and brooch to fall out.

The comb was six inches long and made of ivory with a row of tiny colored beads along the top. Grace held it in her hand, running her finger along the teeth and wondered if it was part of a set and had a brush to match.

The cameo brooch was skillfully carved of coral and ivory and had obviously been designed many years ago. She traced the raised relief, feeling this piece belonged to someone she loved, then offered it to Griff. "What about this? Do you think it belongs to her?"

"Maybe it belongs to you," he said. "Yet another mystery we'll have to unravel."

"You're lucky the miner didn't find that jewelry," Reece said. "I think he would have sold it along with the horse and saddle. You were smart to hide them in that lining and no one would look for a picture in a tobacco pouch. It's obvious you put some thought into what to take with you. Money, sentimental items important to your life, hard tack. I'll say it again, where ever you were headed, you weren't planning on turning back."

"But it doesn't get us any closer to knowing what it all means or who I am, sheriff. I could be an outlaw on the run for all we know."

"In my experience, outlaws usually don't carry a beaded bag and fancy brooch. If you're an outlaw, I'm afraid you're not a very good one," smiled Reece. "I think we need to dig a little deeper before we start making assumptions about your background."

"Well then, where do we go from here?" asked Grace, perplexed as she looked over the bounty spread before them.

Reece picked up the contents of the saddle bag and examined them one at a time, deep in thought. He turned them over in his hands, inspecting each piece as if hoping he could coax a confession of secrets from each one. Then placed them back in the saddle bag.

"I think you should enjoy these treasures and concentrate on those letters A.B.," Reece said, handing Grace the bag. "I got a feeling something is gonna come back to you soon. As far as the letter goes, I don't think there's any way to find the man who wrote it. John is a common name. To find someone with no last name in a city as large like Denver, will be almost impossible."

"He said he was starting a new business. At least that's a clue to his identity, isn't it?" said Griff. "I know it's a long shot but I think it's important enough to try to find him."

"I agree, it's a start," said Reece picking up the letter and reading it again. "The letter isn't dated so we don't know when this happened but if she was carrying it with her, it makes sense it's happened recently. It's possible the sheriff might know of someone new in town that's recently started a business."

He folded the letter and handed it to Grace. "I'll send a message to the sheriff in Denver tomorrow. We'll give him what information we have, which isn't much. He's a good man. He'll do his best to help us out. In the meantime, I've sent a man to Carson City to find the horse and saddle. We'll try to get as much of your life back to you as possible, Grace. Even though it's not much."

"I appreciate everything you're doing, sheriff. You have no idea how much these things mean to me." She grasped the saddle bags in her arms. "This is worth the world to me right now."

Reece smiled and tipped his hat as he rose. "Now, if you'll excuse me, I think Griff and I will go out back and inspect that shed door before I head back to town."

"Will you stay to supper? It's the least I can do after I pointed a gun at you."

"Another time," Reece said, as he rose. "I appreciate the invitation but I know you're anxious to look over the contents of that saddle bag again. I'll take you up on the offer some other day."

The two men headed for the back door and out into the yard, surveying the landscape as they walked. "There's something I wanted to talk to you about that I didn't want Grace to hear."

Griff opened the shed door. He inspected the latch and door frame then stepped inside. "I locked the door on this shed myself before I left this morning. Right after I took the barbed wire cutters. If she didn't open that door then someone else did."

"I figured as much from the look on your face earlier. Has the lock been jimmied? That laundry basket she says she dropped in the middle of the yard was in a different spot when I got back here. I found it sitting on the floor right here in the shed. I'm afraid that bearded cowboy who showed up at Miller's yesterday has discovered Grace is staying here on the Emerald. Looks like our secret is out whether we like it or not."

Griff shook his head in despair rubbing his forehead as he thought. "I should have been more careful. Leaving her alone wasn't a good decision."

"We both should have been smarter," said Reece. "I don't like the idea of these guys moving around the area and us not knowing a thing about them. All we have to go on is her vague description of some man staring through a window. They seem to be a step ahead of us. Showing up here in daylight, this close to the house is a bold move."

"I should have listened to Grace last night when she talked about hearing those voices outside her window. She can't be left alone until we figure out what these guys are after."

The two men maneuvered through the collection of linens and shirts still hanging on the line, shuffling through the grass as they looked for signs of the intruder.

"What do you think she's gotten herself mixed up in, Reece? A girl like her, running off, toting a saddle bag full of trinkets. You think she's running away from home? Might be her family coming after her."

"Well if they are, she's got herself one heck of a family." Reece bent down to pick up a piece of overturned dirt and stared down the hill toward the grazing cattle. "I'd say they were more foe than friend and they'll be back. We need to be ready for them the next time."

"I want you to do everything you can to get that horse back for her," said Griff. "I'll pay whatever it cost. When you find the owner, tell him to name the price. The same goes for the saddle."

"You can count on it," said Reece, smiling wryly. "Nothing will make me happier than to spend your money. In the meantime, do a little yard work back here and cut this grass. No need to give these vermin a place to hide when they come stalking. And fix that clothes line while you're at it. You can't expect a woman to keep your drawers clean with a clothes line hanging on the ground."

"Isn't it about time for you to go home?" Griff grumbled. "I think we've had enough of your insight for one day. Don't be thinking you're coming to supper anytime soon either."

"I don't know how you can stop me, seeing how I already got an invite." Reece flashed an impish smile and tipped his hat. "You worry about keeping Grace safe 'til I return."

"You worry about catching criminals instead of gorging at my dinner table. Make yourself useful and go find that filly," Griff called as Reece mounted his horse and waved before turning toward the road.

He walked back into the house thinking about their conversation. Reece was right. Now that Grace's whereabouts had been discovered, she was still in danger. He planned to ride over to his father's ranch tomorrow morning to get more help for Jesse and devote full time to protecting her.

CHAPTER 6

RETURN OF THE BLACK FILLY

Grace was surprisingly refreshed when she woke early from the first good night's sleep since she was injured. Pulling open the drawer of the night stand, she found the jewelry and letter safe, as if they might have somehow disappeared while she slept.

She reached for the letter and read it again. It was like reading a letter belonging to someone else. There was no emotional attachment to this man named John and she felt no remorse at the dissolution of their relationship. In fact, she was relieved to find she was not married. She wouldn't be able to return to a man she didn't remember, especially after staying at the Emerald.

This letter, containing only one paragraph, brought with it so many questions left unanswered. John, whoever he may be, had mentioned her father. A wonderful piece of information yet, disappointing, for she had no idea where to find him. Griffin and Reece were making a concerted effort to discover her identity but there was no response to their inquiries. Maybe no one knew she was missing, she thought. Maybe no one cared. Was she so distraught at news of her fiancé's change of heart that she left without notice? "You'd think they'd at least miss the horse," she mumbled and tossed the paper to the side.

She thought about the black filly. If only horses could talk. How far had this animal carried her? The sheriff didn't mention any injuries so it seemed the horse had fared better. She wanted this horse and saddle returned quickly, hoping their return would trigger her much needed memories.

She picked up the silk coin purse. Griff was right, it was fancy and she knew it was a memento of happier times. Opening and closing the clasp she tried to imagine when it might have been used. A ball, perhaps. She closed her eyes and tried to visualize herself wearing a beautiful gown and dancing in the arms of a handsome young man and remembered that until recently she had a fiancé. Scrutinizing the situation, her face twisted in a skeptical look as she laid the purse to the side.

She studied the comb and broach, turning them over in her hand. These two items belonged to someone she loved and although they appeared to be useless pieces to drag along, they must have been priceless in her eyes. She wondered if she would ever know their significance.

The tobacco pouch, she was sure, belonged to her father and the portrait, that of her mother. Of all the contents of the saddle bag, she cherished these two pieces the most. Her eyes began to well with tears. Everything laid out before her on the bed were so important that she had hidden them with care, choosing to carry them with her, rather than leaving them in a more secure place, yet, she really had no idea of their meaning. It was so frustrating and so disturbing she was overwhelmed and could not look at them anymore. She gently placed them back in the drawer and climbed out of bed wondering if the others were awake.

Griff hadn't much to say after the sheriff left the day before. He secured the shed door and spent the rest of the available daylight with sickle in hand, slicing through the tall grass, almost skinning the yard until there was not much more than dirt remaining. Somewhat embarrassed at the shabby appearance of the back yard, he sheepishly admitted a bachelor doesn't always consider a coiffed landscape as an important necessity, then tightened the clothes line with the promise to do a better job on upkeep.

It took some prodding for him to admit he found hoof prints down by the pasture but it was impossible to tell whose horse they belonged to and it did not escape her notice when he double checked the locks on all doors and windows while Jesse took one last tour of the yard and buildings before they turned in.

Grace headed for the kitchen hoping she was the first one up. She wanted a chance to make breakfast, feeing it was one more step on the road to recovery. Finding no sign of Griffin or Jesse, she stoked the fire in the stove and looked around for the ingredients she would need.

Biscuits and gravy sounded good although she thought it wise to gather eggs before starting. Thinking twice, she looked out the window toward the back of the house. She was relieved to find nothing disturbed since yesterday when Griff had finished cleaning up but left the door locked, and walked to the front room.

The chicken coup was located by the barn, which seemed like a long walk at the time. She took a deep breath, thinking of how it felt yesterday when she heard that shed door slamming and questioned whether it was wise to leave the house. She took another deep breath followed by a loud grunt, disgusted with herself for being scared to open the door. She would never get over this constant fear if she didn't push herself to be brave and the best way to do that was to go

Grace looked disappointed as she continued. "I came upon some water. A stream or perhaps a lake. I guess it's a little fuzzy, now. I stopped to let the horse drink. Everything around me was so still. Not a sound. No birds chirping, not a leaf moving. But the strangest part about it all is that even in the silence around me I heard a voice whispering in my ear. A man's voice. A soft, sweet, gentle voice that kept urging me onward. 'Run, they're coming', he said and I knew I needed to keep going at all costs."

"Well, I'd say that was quite a dream," said Jesse, sipping his coffee. "but I must admit it sounds like you just threw bits of facts together from things you are familiar with already. Tall grass from the back yard, the filly Reece talked about, the only clothes you remember. I'm sorry Gracie but seems these are memories already stored in your head and they came out in the form of this dream."

"Jesse," Griff complained, shaking his head in disgust. "You sure know how to ruin a good breakfast. You're not doing much to encourage her."

"Well I'm sorry but I'm just speaking my mind," answered Jesse, defensively. "I hope for Grace's sake it does mean something." He reached across the table and squeezed her hand. "I don't mean to be so negative. I want nothing more than for you to get your memory back and reunite with your family. I guess maybe this old man doesn't know when to keep his mouth shut."

"It's alright, Jesse" Grace said, smiling half-heartedly. "I want this so badly I'm just talking myself into believing the dream is relevant."

"I disagree with Jesse," said Griff, sending a stern look at his friend. "Yes, your dream has many familiar pieces but this is the first positive dream you've had and it seems that for once you've been able to put these scraps of information together in a story that makes sense with what we know might have happened. You remembered a hat and that fact hasn't come up before. No one has ever mentioned a lake or pond or whatever you saw so if you ask me, that's a new memory and this man's voice you hear isn't the gruff talk of the men who hurt you. All in all, I think it was very insightful and I suspect you'll be having more of them."

"He's right, Gracie," said Jesse, nodding his head in agreement. "I hadn't looked at it that way and what he says makes a whole lot of sense. It was a good dream and I was wrong not to recognize it."

Grace smiled contently, pleased with what Griff had said and Jesse's apology for misjudging. She agreed with Griff that is was a breakthrough and was sure that, even though the objects in the saddle bag weren't yet familiar, they, none the less, had stirred these memories hidden deep within her subconscious.

"Gracie, looks like it's going to be the two of us this morning while Griff heads over to see his father. I think we can survive without him, don't you?"

Griff could tell by the look on her face that she was apprehensive and thought twice about making the trip. "I can stay here if you like."

"No, I wouldn't think of it. Jesse and I will be fine. Maybe I can help him with his work." She looked at Jesse ready for him to moan at the thought of her tagging along being of no use, but he beamed at her and chuckled. "I can't think of a thing I'd enjoy more. You go on about your business and leave this young lady and me to take charge. Spending time outside has been good for her." He frowned and looked apologetic. Except for yesterday, I guess."

"Take charge," snickered Griff. "That's a scary thought. Hang on to that shot gun Grace and if there's any sign of trouble get back to the house and lock the doors."

"I will," she answered with a serious face. "I'm sure I'll be alright."

"I'll head out after breakfast and be back as soon as I can."

The morning was filled with chores but by afternoon Grace and Jesse had accomplished more than either thought possible. She was content with her time outside. It put her in a good mood and for a while she was happy and forgot the past weeks. Jesse told her of Griff's plans to enlarge his herd in the coming year. Horses were in demand and selling for a solid price if they were from good stock and Griffin had learned how to breed good horses from his older brother who was, himself, known for raising quality animals. Jesse and Griff both thought it was time they made that investment.

Grace marveled at the way the older man spoke of his young friend's knowledge and his love for this land and praised his father, Tom, for raising a hard-working son like Griff.

"I'm not sure Tom Kelly gave his son enough credit for having the talent to make this ranch succeed but neither Griff nor his father realize they are alike in many ways. Both have always had the dream of building a ranch into something to be proud of. And, I might add, willing to make sacrifices to achieve their goal. Tom is a good friend and I can tell you he has made sacrifices through the years, some of which he had no control over.

Grace found herself wanting to be around to see Griff's dream unfold and wondered how this story would end. She was fond of him and thought him to be a kind person in showing such concern for her and she wondered how long she could take advantage of his hospitality.

"Looks like you have a surprise coming," said Jesse as he looked toward the road that led to the ranch. "There's Reece heading through the gate leading another horse. I wouldn't be surprised if that fine animal didn't belong to you."

Grace followed Jesse's eyes as she watched the sheriff reach the barn with a black filly following behind. She walked out to greet him, her eyes dancing with excitement as she reached to take the animal's lead.

"She's beautiful," Grace said as she scratched the horse's forehead. "I wonder if she remembers me better than I do her."

"I'm sure she does," Reece smiled, dismounting. "My deputy found her in Carson City. She was purchased by a man who resides there and your little filly has been living a life of luxury with plenty of hay and a good grooming. It's easy to see she's been well taken care of. I guess I should tell you that Griff paid a pretty penny to get her back along with the promise of a comparable horse for the man who purchased her from the miner. I need to give him his just dues for making her return possible."

"I am amazed at how good he is to me and how both of you are trying to make this right."

"Well, it's not really that surprising to me. He's a good person and I think he has a vested interest in all of this. The making you happy part, I mean."

She looks healthy to me," Grace said as they walked around the horse together checking her legs and hoofs for injuries. "I'm glad she found her way to a good home."

"She'll need to be shoed. I can stop by and take care of that for you, if you like," said Reece. "You want to go for a ride. It's a good way for you two to get to know each other again."

"I'd love to but maybe not too far. I promised Griffin I would stick with Jesse today. He went to speak to his father."

"Jesse, do you think we could saddle this fine stead for a little ride," asked Reece. "I think Grace is anxious to see how she does and I'm hoping it might jog some memories."

"Please," Grace asked with begging eyes.

"I guess it would be alright," said Jesse. "I agree that you shouldn't stay too long. I don't want Griff coming home and worried about where you've gone, even if you're with Reece. He's had enough worry already."

Once saddled Grace and Reece headed for the road and through the lush spring pastures. The horse felt like a natural fit as they meandered through the fields, most of which she had never seen before. Griffin had kept her close to the house and she was in awe at the beautiful ranch he owned. She thought of her conversation with Jesse about his plans to make it as wonderful as the one he was raised on.

"She's responding well to you," Reece finally said after a time. "I guess she does remember you. I thought we might ride into town sometime. Maybe we could get your filly shoed at the blacksmith's while we're there and have lunch at the hotel." He gave Grace his best smile hoping to persuade her to accept her offer. "It would be a nice change for the day."

"I'd love to go to town. It would be exciting to eat at a big hotel and it would give me the opportunity to visit Miller Mercantile again and thank Juanita for helping me with shopping. We rushed off so quickly the last time, I hardly had a chance to say goodbye. Griff was supposed to show me around that day but, of course, that man in the window ruined all of that."

I can come back tomorrow if you want. We can make a day of it. I might even introduce you to some of the town folk. The Spencers and Fergusons and my deputy. They've all been asking about you and been pretty worried."

"The Spencers who are Griff's friends? He's told me about them. I'd love to meet them. They seem like good people to know. I think we better head back, now."

"There's a social coming up, too."

"A social?" Grace said, surprised. "Oh, I'm not sure I'm ready for that."

Returning to the house they found Griff sitting on the porch swing stewing. He was disappointed that Reece had brought the horse back when he wasn't home. He wanted to be the one to ride with Grace when she rode the filly for the first time. He had missed that opportunity and resented his friend for taking her without him.

"Griff, Reece brought my horse back. Isn't that wonderful? I've fallen in love with her," said Grace excitedly. "Reece says she'll need to be shoed. I've already taken her riding."

"If she needs to be shoed, I'll take care of it," Griff snapped, as he walked off the porch, lifted a front leg of the animal and inspected its hoof. "I'm smart enough to know how to care for a horse. It's my job to do those things as long as you're under my care."

"The sheriff wants to take me to town tomorrow to have lunch at the hotel. We were going to the blacksmith's. I wanted to speak to Mrs. Miller." Grace looked at Griff with wishful eyes but could tell by his expression that he wasn't pleased with the idea.

"You're not thinking clearly, Reece," said Griff as he glared at the sheriff. "Considering how things went the last time, it's not the best idea." He looked at Grace's downcast face and shook his head. "I won't stand in your way if that's what you want."

"You can't keep her hidden here forever," Reece said. "I thought we were going to take her out in public with hope someone would recognize her. Besides, someone is already stalking around this place. There's no saying she's any safer staying at this ranch."

"I already said she can do what she wants. It's not my decision and you know how I feel about it," Griff snapped, throwing one arm in the air, dismissively.

"I'd like to remind you both that I won't be wrangled over like a scrap of meat," Grace interrupted, indignantly as the two men halted their conversation which was growing more heated by the minute.

"I appreciate the offer, sheriff." She looked at Reece with a half-hearted smile, making it apparent she was disappointed. "It was kind of you to ask."

"But," she continued, with a stern look toward Griffin who glanced away when their eyes met. "I believe it's best to stay here. Another time maybe."

"I'm holding you to it," said Reece. "In fact, I look forward to it. Since Griff won't let me take you to town and show you off then I'd like to take your horse."

"My horse?" Not sure if the sheriff was joking, Grace looked at Griff for an answer. If Reece was serious, she was sure Griff would object. She just got the filly back and hated to see her taken away so quickly. Griff glanced at her but said nothing.

"I think it might be a way of flushing out these men," said Reece. "I've heard from the marshal in Carson City. Three men showed up there a couple of days ago asking questions about the horse. Right after my deputy picked her up. They put a lot of pressure on the gentleman we bought her from. Seems they wanted answers about the miner and where exactly the horse had been found in the first place. They asked the gentleman if anything else was found with the horse. All this questioning spooked the gentleman who notified the marshal, but not before the gentleman told these men that the miner sold the saddle to a separate buyer. All three men left town before the marshal could question them. I believe the gentleman was glad he sold your filly. He didn't want a run-in with those men."

"Did this gentleman happen to catch a name or give a description of what they looked like?" Griff asked. He realized where Reece was going with this plan. As much as he wanted to catch these guys, the last thing he wanted was for them to be sneaking about the area again.

"One was an older man. Maybe your pa's age. The other two were in their twenties. About like us. Dirty looking bunch from what the gentleman said. He was leery of asking too many questions so didn't get a name, but the marshal is still asking around hoping to find someone else who may have come in contact with them so, like I said, I've got this idea."

Grace stiffened at the mention of the three men and she sat with a panicked look as Reece outlined his plan for her beautiful black horse. She hated the idea of her horse being used for bait to trap these vicious men intent on harming her. She'd sooner things be left alone as they were with hope they would never return. The thought that the horse might be taken away so quickly was disheartening.

"I want to try to draw these men out," Reece continued. "I'll take the horse back to town and tie her in front of places like the Elkhorn Saloon, livery and maybe the bank, or even Miller's. The men haven't been shy about showing up and if they recognize her, they may ask questions. Once they show themselves, we'll be waiting for them."

"I see your point, Reece and know you're right," said Griff begrudgingly. "It's a good idea and has a chance of working. Maybe only for a couple of days. For Grace's sake. She just got the horse back. If they don't show their face by the end of the week, then I want you to promise to bring her back. Maybe the saddle will be here by then and that will tell us something."

"There's still the offer to let me take you to town for the day. You can visit her then," Reece said smiling. He glanced slyly at Griff who snarled at him.

"The only female you're taking to town is the that filly," Griff snapped. "Be happy with that. You have a week before I'm coming to get her back."

Grace agreed to relinquish the horse and stood sadly watching as Reece rode away. She was torn about the idea of using the horse as bait. She wanted the three men to show up and give Reece the chance to capture them but the thought of them finding their way to the ranch again was unsettling. The next couple of days would be an uneasy time and she gave Griff a foreboding look as they walked back to the house.

"Don't worry," he said softly, trying to muster a smile. "Your horse is safe with Reece. If those men set one foot in the county, he'll find them."

She smiled timidly as they climbed the step. Even with all that had gone on, she found it charming that Reece and Griffin might be at odds over her attentions and wondered if her life would ever again be so simple that she might allow herself to enjoy the company of two handsome men in a more pleasant time.

CHAPTER 7

Unexpected Visitor

A week had gone by with no one showing their face in town looking for the black filly or the girl who owned her. There was a moment of anticipation when Reece was positive he had Grace's assailants caught in his trap after discovering the horse missing from the post in front of the bank where it had been tied all morning. However, it was only a short time before the bank president, Horatio Ferguson, who was unaware of the sheriff's plan, confessed he had grown tired of watching the animal through his office window and ordered it taken to the livery until claimed by the owner. Reece's plan appeared to be failing and he was at a loss for how to draw the men out.

Grace continued to improve both physically and emotionally. She spent time each morning reading the letter from her former fiancé, John, and inspecting the other items from the saddle bag. Holding each tightly in her hand, she tried to gleam their significance in her life, but they would not reveal their secrets so she would carefully rewrap each piece, then place them in the nightstand drawer for safe keeping, next to a revolver Griff had given her.

The dreams continued with the same recurring theme but each one revealed more detail. The horse galloping as she was being chased, the need to escape then drawn to the water. Colors were vibrant and scenery clearer. The rose design etched into the saddle bag was now a dominant image. Why was the water at the clearing of the trees so important, she wondered? There was never an answer.

Her fears subsided as the days moved on and with no further sightings of the bearded cowboy or disturbing noises in the night, she could relax. She ventured out to the back yard by herself on laundry day, but always within ear shot of Griff or Jesse. These were peaceful days and Grace hoped they were a sign that the men who harmed her had given up.

Griff and Jesse took turns going to town to get a daily update, but the only news Reece offered was a message from the marshal in Carson City informing him that the saddle was located in Denver. Today, Griff had gone to see Reece to ask, at Grace's request, if he might bring her filly back to the ranch and she was anxious for his return.

The sight of an unfamiliar buggy entering the gate by the road brought more curiosity than fear as she peered out the window watching it approach the house. No outsider except Reece had visited the ranch and she glanced toward the barn, hoping to spot Jesse. A young lady climbed the steps and knocked. Grace hesitated for a moment before opening the door to greet her.

The girl was in her twenties and quite attractive with dark hair and blue eyes. It was obvious she spared no expense on her wardrobe as she confidently entered the room with a swish of her dress and rustle of petticoats. Looking around, the young woman flashed a warm smile.

Grace suddenly felt drab in her plain dress and primped her hair, trying to improve her appearance as she shyly smiled. "Is there something I can do for you?"

"Where's Griff?" The woman walked to the kitchen and peeked in. "He asked me to stop by and help you."

"He's gone to town," Grace replied, with a look of concern, her eyes following the young woman as she sat down in the leather chair. "What is it that you're to help with?"

"He asked me to bring a few things you might need. Combs, hair pins, some ribbon and a locket you're welcome to borrow. I find it looks nice with almost any dress. What do you plan to wear tomorrow evening?"

Grace twirled strands of hair around her fingers, looking at her simple clothing and shrugged her shoulders. "I'm afraid I'm confused. What am I to do tomorrow evening?"

"The social, of course. Didn't Griff tell you? Honestly, that man. It's a wonder he gets along without me." She shook her head and chuckled. "I guess I shouldn't be shocked he left you totally in the dark about my visit."

"Social?" Grace asked, wondering who this woman was and what her real purpose for being there might be. "Sorry, but I'm still confused."

"I can see that. I'm talking about the church social. Box lunches, horseshoes, usually a pie eating contest or some such thing and a dance in the evening. Everyone in town attends. Griff, me, Jesse."

"Oh yes, the social. The sheriff mentioned something about it."

"I'm sure he did," the woman snickered. "Griff thought you should go and I do too. We both think you've been cooped up here too long."

Grace was not interested in anything this woman had to say and stared as she nonchalantly sat in the chair. Here was this pretty girl, who obviously knew Griff well, assigned to the job of making her look presentable for a church social. She was hurt that he felt she needed help and envious of this young woman who meant something to him. It was silly of her not to realize before that he might already have his eye set on another woman. She was unprepared for this first meeting.

"And Griff will be taking you?" she said timidly, suddenly feeling very small and out of place.

"Heavens no," the woman replied, rolling her eyes. "I'd sooner die than go to the social with my brother."

"Your brother. Griff is your brother?" Grace smiled at the misunderstanding and couldn't help showing her pleasure at this news. "I apologize I didn't realize this. You're Rachel."

"Of course. Who else would I be? I feel that I'm the one who needs to apologize. I guess I should have introduced myself but I thought that crazy brother of mine would have told you I was coming. No wonder you've been looking at me so strangely." Rachel shook her head and laughed. "I can imagine what you must have thought. I'm sorry Griff didn't inform you of his plans. It's like he thinks a woman can read his mind. He's taking you of course and asked me to stop by to see if there was something you need. He feels a little guilty that your trip to Miller's was cut short when that horrid man showed up. Everyone is talking about it. I can't imagine what I would have done. Probably just died right there on the spot."

"I felt like I might do that, at the time," Grace sighed. "Everyone is talking about it? What exactly are they saying?"

"Well, not everyone," Rachel giggled. "I may have exaggerated a bit. Griff has been closed-mouth about it all. He's hardly said a thing, which is why I couldn't wait to meet you today. Margaret wanted to come too but my brother put his foot down about that. Seems he's afraid those men will come back. Honestly, he's such a worrier."

"Margaret?"

"Margaret Spencer. I suppose he hasn't mentioned a thing about the Spencers either. If I didn't know better I'd say he wanted you all to himself. "

"Well he has been concerned but he did tell me about Will and Margaret Spencer and of course his family. In his defense, it has been a little frightening for me."

"Well don't you worry. My pa says those men are probably long gone and if they do show up, we have an army of friends and family ready to protect you. And don't worry about Margaret either. She's organizing the garden club for a get-together. You'll be the guest of honor, of course. They're all about to bust with excitement over meeting you. As soon as Griffin gives the word, it's on to the Spencer's even if we have to call out the cavalry for an escort. Our meetings are quite famous. It'll be fun."

Rachel suddenly jumped up and glanced around the room again. "In the meantime, let's look at what you have. I threw a few things in a trunk you might like but, of course, don't feel obligated..."

"No, that's wonderful," Grace squealed as she followed Rachel into the bedroom. "I don't have many things to wear so whatever you've brought will be fine."

Any resentment Grace initially felt toward Rachel melted away as the two sifted through a trunk full of clothes to find the perfect dress for her debut at the church social. Just to talk to another woman her age who was sympathetic to her situation restored her spirits more than she could have imagined. Rachel's entertaining acumen of local society fascinated her as she sat on the front porch with her new friend, once again wondering about her past and if there was a similar cohort she had forgotten along with everyone else.

"I brought cookies," Rachel said, pulling back the linen cloth covering a small round basket she was juggling on her lap. "My secret recipe and you'll love them. They're Griff's favorite."

Their minds had been synchronized on almost every detail of the events surrounding her situation and how to proceed on the capture of the men who were chasing her.

"Do they compete with each other about everything?"

"Women mostly, but I think it goes deeper than that." She put down the glass of tea and picked up another cookie from the basket. Grace wondered how she could eat so much and still be able to fit into the buggy.

"Reece's father drank. It's only out of friendship that I don't say outright that the man was a drunk. Reece was an only child. Some say his mother lost other children during pregnancy because Mr. Cameron had a bad temper and took it out on his wife.

The Camerons didn't have much money, due to the fact that Reece's pa spent more time in the Elkhorn Saloon then he did working his land. Reece ate many meals at our house. It broke my mama's heart to see the situation he was in and the way he and his mother were treated. Pa went to the Cameron ranch and had it out with Mr. Cameron a couple of times about how he should be taking care of Reece and his ma and not spending all his money on liquor and women at the Elkhorn but it never did any good.

One January night when Reece was about fourteen, Mr. Cameron stumbled out of the saloon and passed out in the alley by Miller Mercantile. He was never home much so no one missed him for three days. By the time Reece came to town looking for him, he was already dead. You would think that might be a good thing but it made it more difficult for Reece. He was solely responsible for his mother's welfare. He would have quit school to work the farm but my pa and some of the others in town wouldn't hear of it. Griff and Matt and some of the other boys took turns going over after school and helped with chores. Pa made sure what few cattle they had made it to market each year and, I suspect, paid Reece more than they were worth. Mrs. Cameron passed away the spring before ma died. I don't know which was harder for Reece. I think he always looked at mama as a second mother."

Rachel's face grew solemn as she took another drink from her glass and drew a deep breath. "I feel like Reece has always envied Griff. You probably realize the Kelly children haven't wanted for much. Our parents were devoted to each other and ranchers from all around the state seek out my pa's advice when it comes to cattle. Reece, as the sheriff, has earned the respect of people in town. He makes good money and built a nice house on his land but I believe he still carries the shame of his childhood."

"He always seems so confident, Grace replied. "He's very polite although he can be a bit standoffish as if he doesn't want to get too close to a person. Do they fight over all women?"

"No," Rachel laughed. "Only the ones worth fighting over. There's nothing those two won't do to get a leg up on the other when it comes to females. If one finds a girl he thinks is attractive, the other figures out a way to court her. Honestly, it's difficult to keep score. I think it's why neither is married. Mama use to say some day they would both find the right girl and settle down. Poor Pa always declared that he would be dead and buried before he saw grandchildren. Thank goodness Matt found a wife and had a baby. Little Hope has brought so much joy to our family."

"Have another cookie," Rachel offered, handing the basket to Grace.

"Thank you but I need to save some room for supper." Grace held up her hand and waved off Rachel's efforts. "I expect Griff any minute and he'll want to eat right away."

"Tell Griff to look me up tomorrow at the social. I'm going with Bart Ferguson. He's been a beau of mine for a couple of years. Lance, my younger brother, can never make up his mind about a girl. He's a lot like Griff in that way. I guess he'll be going alone. You'll find Reece with a flock of women trailing behind him. As I've already said, women seem to swoon when he's around."

Rachel rolled her eyes with a disgusted groan. "Then there's Clara Richter but I don't have the strength for her today. Some other time."

She put down the glass and looked toward the gate. "There's Griff riding up. Wait until I give him a piece of my mind for not telling you about the social. Sometimes I don't know how he'll ever get a woman to take him serious."

"No, don't. It doesn't matter if he forgot," said Grace as she watched Rachel start down the porch steps. I think it's nice that he wants to take me. Please don't make a fuss."

"Well, if that's what you want," Rachel said with a smile, grabbing one last cookie before waving to her brother as she climbed into the buggy. "You may need to box his ears once or twice to make him behave. Looks like he's leading another horse. That should make up for his faults. We'll talk more tomorrow."

"It's my filly. He's brought her back."

Grace waited for Griff to tie both horses to the post. She was anxious to hear the news from town. Reece had already mentioned something about the return of the saddle. Griff thought it curious the saddle had ended up in the same town as Grace's fiancé' but decided not to dwell on the subject with her. It was to arrive by stage in a few days.

Walking in the house, Griffin saw remnants of Rachel's visit. There were petticoats draped over chairs, hair ribbons laying on a table and the contents of a sewing basket strewn on the floor. Embarrassed that her undergarments were in plain view, Grace quickly snatched them up and into the bedroom with apologies for the clutter.

"So, I see you met my little sister," Griff called after Grace as she left the room.

"Yes, it was quite a treat and definitely unexpected," she called back. "She left a basket full of your favorite cookies. I think that's sweet."

"Sweet," Griff said, making a sour face. "They're enough to give a bull indigestion. I sometimes think she's trying to kill me. Did she force you to eat them?"

"Honestly," Grace scolded as she entered the room again. "What a thing to say. It was a nice gesture and of course she offered them to me. They were quite tasty." Grace plastered on a faint smile as she spoke. "They have an unusual taste."

"Admit it, they're awful. The only thing they should be used for is skeet shooting."

Grace frowned at Griff for a moment then started to giggle which turned in to a burst of laughter, tears running down her cheeks. "You're right, they are awful. This was such a nice thing for her to do but the first bite stuck to the roof of my mouth so hard I thought I was going to need a shovel to dig it out. I'm such a terrible person for thinking that. She said it was her secret recipe."

"You're not terrible," Griff said, laughing loudly. "It's a recipe she needs to keep secret. It fact, it's been a family secret for years. "Don't ever mention a thing to her. She tries so hard to make us happy and it would crush her to know how we really feel. Just make sure you have plenty of water on hand if she offers one again. What else did you girls do today?"

"She was kind enough to help me with a dress for tomorrow evening," said Grace, turning serious again. "You remember tomorrow evening, don't you Griffin?"

The smile faded from Griff's face as he suddenly remembered the church social and how, in his hurry to go to town, had forgotten to tell Grace he would be taking her. He looked down at the table with remorse in his eyes and shook his head.

"I'm sorry. I had other things on my mind and I've been busy with the chores."

"I'm not mad, Grace said. "Well, maybe I was a little at first, but only because I had no idea who Rachel was, walking into the house. She was showing me hair combs and lockets and asking about my clothes."

"I wanted to tell you myself and I'm sorry if Rachel spoiled things for you. I knew you were disappointed about not getting to eat lunch in town and I thought this might be fun. Rachel wanted to meet you and asked if she could stop by. I know how you women are about wearing the right dress and fixing your hair a certain way for these things and trust me, no one knows how to spend endless hours worrying about that stuff better than my sister."

Griff, raised a finger as if making a point that would silence any arguments, while Grace gave him a scornful look. "Not that you women shouldn't spend time fixing your hair, because men certainly enjoy looking at a pretty woman."

He dropped his hand in defeat, with an exasperated sigh. "I thought you might like to meet new people. We can dance if you want and have a picnic. Mrs. Bernard makes the best apple pie in three counties."

"Do you think Mrs. Bernard's apple pie is better than mine?" Grace stood stoically with a stern face. She enjoyed watching Griffin squirm a little and remembered what Rachel said about having to box his ears to make him behave.

"I've never tasted your pie," Griff said sheepishly, knowing this was a test but not sure of the correct answer to the question. "But I'm sure when you make one it will outdo Mrs. Bernard's one hundred percent."

"Then I shall make one for you. Right after we take the horses for a ride. I'm so happy I've got her back."

"If that will make up for forgetting to tell you about the social then I'm ready."

"When we come back I might make you some of Rachel's cookies."

"No please, Griff moaned in agony. "Not the cookies. Anything but those cookies."

CHAPTER 8

A Social Event

The burgundy satin was much too fancy for a church social, in Grace's opinion, but she was assured that only widows and young girls would show up in anything less. It was more elaborate than anything she would have picked on her own. The black lace perfectly trimmed the scoop neckline and around the cuffs of the sleeves. It required some alteration. Rachel, although a thin woman, was shapelier through the hips and bust so the bodice needed to be tightened an inch or two.

Grace slept well past the hour when she usually woke. Not surprising since she was up late trying on the dress Rachel let her borrow. She couldn't resist trying it on once more before heading to the kitchen for breakfast. She kept turning around to see the small bustle in the mirror which, according to her new friend, was the height of fashion although she found it difficult to sit down when wearing one.

Underneath was a black satin underskirt also trimmed in black lace and, also on loan. Apparently, it wouldn't do to wear a plain white petticoat so once again Rachel came to the rescue with just the right garment. It was amazing how many clothes she was able to stuff in the trunk she carried in her buggy and might rival Miller Mercantile if it were all to be inventoried. Grace loved the way she felt in the dress and thought she might look suitable for the Kelly clan after all.

Only Jesse was sitting at the table by the time she dressed and entered the kitchen which was good because he would be easy to shoo away so she could start her daily cleaning. She wanted to finish her housework early and have plenty of time to get ready for the evening. Jesse promised to bring her two chickens to fry for the box lunch and she planned to prepare some potatoes and a new recipe for biscuits Rachel had given her. They were supposedly a favorite of Griffin's but she said that about the cookies too.

"Where did Griff go so early?" Grace poured the last of the coffee and sat down. "I hope he hasn't gone off some place and forgotten about the social again."

"He went over to his pa's ranch to pick up their buggy. It's better than that old one we've got and he wanted something nice to take you to the dance tonight. Seems like a lot of fuss for a church social if you ask me. Of course, Tom won't be using it. He's not much for socials since Eleanor passed."

"That's disappointing. I was hoping to get a chance to meet him this evening. What was Mrs. Kelly like?" Grace asked, tearing off a piece of biscuit and spreading it with butter.

"A beautiful woman and the kindest human being I've ever known. She came from around Boston. Cambridge, I think it was. You probably didn't know that Tom was a sea captain. He met Eleanor at a dinner party and was smitten the minute he saw her. Ben Griffin, her daddy, was high society. What they use to call old money. He was not about to let some brash, wild, young seaman marry his daughter, but Tom wouldn't give up. He practically camped outside their front door until the old man gave in. Once they were married, Tom didn't want to leave his young bride and go back to sea so he packed up what little possessions they had, said goodbye to Boston and headed west. You can imagine what her family thought of that. Despite her gentile ways, Eleanor was as strong willed as Tom and she was determined to make a home out west with her husband. I think it's what made them so perfect together."

"Is that when you met them? When they came to Nevada?" Grace stuffed the biscuit in her mouth and followed with a drink of coffee.

Jesse smiled as he reminisced about their early days. "I was busting broncos around Carson City when Tom and Eleanor came through. They were a sorry sight, that's for sure. He had just bought his first piece of land and was in town to file the deed. She was in a family way by that time, expecting Matthew and wasn't much help to him on that little scrap of land they called a ranch. They weren't giving up though. No, sir, they sure weren't."

Jesse picked up his empty cup and looked around. "Any more of that coffee?"

"No, sorry. I can make some more if you want. It won't take long. She opened a tin and measured the coffee, pouring the grounds into a small muslin bag, tied it with a string and dipped it in the pot of hot water sitting on the stove.

"I couldn't leave Tom to do all that work on his own with fall weather and a baby coming, so I decided to stay until spring and give him a hand until he could get his cattle to market and afford to hire some men. Of course, once I tasted Eleanor's cooking, I wasn't going anywhere. That was the beginning of a lifelong friendship." Jesse chuckled to himself. "At least so far."

Grace filled Jesse's cup with steaming coffee and he took a sip. "We built a cabin that was barely big enough for one, let alone a man, his wife and a child. I spent that first winter sleeping in the barn but I didn't mind bunking out there.

Every couple of years we were building on a room for another baby. Griff came next. He's named after Eleanor's father, you know. That seemed to patch things up with the old man. Benjamin Griffin Kelly, but somehow calling him Griff just seemed to stick.

Little Rachel was the prettiest baby I ever saw." Jesse grabbed his right index finger with his left hand and tightly squeezed, holding it up for Grace to see. "Her little hand would wrap around my finger so tight and not let go. No wonder she's such a pistol today."

Lance," Jesse laughed and shook his head. "He was the chubbiest baby I've ever seen. You wouldn't know it to look at him now. He was Eleanor's child, that's for sure and so much like her. When he came along, they found themselves with a full house and running out of room. Tom had a talent for raising cattle and we did well. He kept buying land and finally built that big monstrosity of a house for his family. Eleanor set about making sure their home and Tom had the style and manners fitting for a gentleman of his growing status. He was rough around the edges at first but now I guess he folds his napkin about as well as the rest of them."

"Oh, Jesse," Grace laughed. "She must have taught you something too. I've seen your folded napkins."

"Well no one else was about to do it. I never married, so Tom and his family were the only ones I had and they are like my flesh and blood. Every one of those kids is like my own."

"Seems like the Kelly family spends a lot of time taking in strays like you and me." She watched Jesse wipe a tear from the corner of his eye.

"Yes, they do," Jesse said, grinning as he stood. "And if we don't get our chores done for today, you and I will be looking for a new place to roost come sundown." He patted her on the shoulder as he walked out. "I'll be in the barn if you need me. Just holler when you're ready for those chickens."

It was noon before Griffin returned from the Kelly ranch driving the four-passenger surrey on loan from his father. The large carriage, looked to Grace, like something fit for a queen. It was crafted from walnut and polished to a glossy shine. The seats were leather and the canopy top, made of brown canvas, had matching fringe that fluttered when the wind blew.

Griff also borrowed two majestic, chestnut horses with freshly brushed manes and manicured hooves. He'd spent all morning grooming them and as they pranced proudly past the barn, Jesse grumbled that it was all a waste of a good morning's work.

"I think they're wonderful," Grace said, clapping her hands as Griff jumped down and bowed deeply.

"Your chariot awaits, fair princess."

"Not before I wash off some of this barnyard smell I've accumulated today," she laughed. "I'm thankful to Rachel for letting me borrow her burgundy dress. I wouldn't have done your carriage and team justice if I wore anything less. Now go and let me finish my work."

⅄

Grace emptied the bucket of warm water into the tub. Immersing her arm to the elbow, she stirred and, being satisfied with its temperature, tipped the glass bottle containing the lavender oil, sideways, watching it slowly drain. She gracefully slipped in and sat down, sighing as she leaned back and relaxed.

Submerging a pitcher, she smiled as her thoughts went back to the grand carriage and chestnut horses ready to carry them to the social and for a moment she did not care about anything else going on in her life. It had already been a beautiful day with the promise of a beautiful evening. The chicken was fried, potatoes cooked, blackberry cobbler baked and all packed carefully into a basket along with table service and a small blanket she found when cleaning. She wanted this evening to be perfect.

She raised the pitcher and poured the warm water over her head and down her shoulders. Grabbing the soap, she lathered her hair, enjoying the peaceful moment alone when her sanctuary was interrupted by banging on the door.

"If you don't want me going to this social smelling like the back end of a steer, you might want to finish up in there," Griff said loudly. "Jesse wants to wash off some top soil too."

"That's impossible. I've just started so you'll have to wait," Grace yelled back, sliding lower into the tub to rinse her hair, determined to stake claim to her territory. "You can't expect me to look nice if I don't have time to get ready."

"We're never gonna get there if you don't get out of that tub. We're not meeting the president," Griffin said in an exasperated voice.

"I told you it was a lot of fuss for a social," mumbled Jesse as he walked by, shaking his head.

"She wants to look nice," whispered Griff. "She's planned all day."

"Well I'm not the one beating down the door. Where's my good shirt?"

"It's just a church social, Grace." Griff called through the door then turned to Jesse and pointed. "Try the store room."

"I want to make a good impression and I'm not showing up looking like a hired cook," Grace shouted back. "I'll just be a few more minutes"

"You will never look like the hired anything and you forget I have a sister. I'm not fooled one bit with that 'only a few more minutes' statement. If you're not out in fifteen minutes, I'll bust down the door and drag you out," he said, looking at Jesse and raising his eyebrows with a devilish grin."

Grace shot up from the water with a gasp. "You wouldn't dare, Griffin Kelly. Jesse would shoot you."

"Jesse wants in too. You'll get no help from him." Griff knocked on the door once more. "Fifteen minutes, Grace." he said as he walked away. "I guess I'll go soak in the horse trough."

Feeling guilty, Grace begrudgingly grabbed a towel and climbed out of the tub. She frowned dejectedly as she stared in the mirror at her dripping hair wondering what to do. Rachel suggested curls and offered heat tongs but that didn't seem to suit. She wanted to wear her hair down but it wouldn't be flattering with the dress. Scooping up her drenched locks she twisted her hair as she piled it on her head and imagined a French Braid held tight in the back with one of Rachel's silver combs. She looked at her reflection with approval and threw a towel on her head before sneaking back to the bedroom.

Once dressed and satisfied with her appearance, Grace made one more circle in front of the mirror before joining Griff and Jesse in the front room. She blushed when her eyes met Griff's as he leaned against the mantle, grinning broadly, taken aback by the sight of this young woman who had blossomed into a beautiful flower. He took her hand and she slowly twirled while Jesse whistled with approval.

"Gracie, I believe you'll be the prettiest girl at the dance," said Jesse. "If this young man isn't careful I may steal you away."

"You said we were making too much fuss over a social," Griff laughed. "Now you're all sunshine and compliments."

"Well who wouldn't be, after seeing this beautiful young lady. I guess I wasn't thinking too clearly before. Wait there a minute Gracie and I'll go saddle old Ned and take you on over to the dance."

"Go saddle old Ned," grumbled Griff. "That would be a sight." He winked at his friend as he led Grace, picnic basket in hand, to the carriage and headed for the church social.

"Now, we don't have to stay," said Griff when they arrived. He reached for Grace's hand, helping her down as she scanned the field before them which was buzzing with excitement.

"Why wouldn't we want to stay?" answered Grace. Despite the cheery expression, she was a bit nervous at the sight of so many people and for a moment wished they were back in the safety of the ranch house.

"I see they've already started the three-legged race." Griff pointed to a hill where both adults and children, paired off, awkwardly trying to run with one leg tied to the other's. "My brother, Matt, and I use to win all the time when we were kids. Once, I lost my footing and fell but Matt didn't even stop. He just dragged me along, bouncing on the ground 'til we got to the finish line."

"We're you hurt?" asked Grace, trying not to laugh.

"Only my pride."

"And those men over there? What are they up to?" Grace grabbed Griff's arm as they passed a party of young men gathered under a tree, sharing a silver flask and ogling women.

"Well..."Griff hesitated. "I guess they're having a political discussion."

Grace tightened her grip as she watched the men mumble to each other then suddenly erupt in loud snickers as a female strolled by.

"Don't worry," Griff said, patting her hand in assurance. "They're harmless."

"There's Sheriff Cameron." Grace excitedly waved at Reece when she spotted him talking with two women. He waved back causing the women to turn a critical eye toward her, whispering as she and Griff drew near. Their catty behavior made her feel as if her face was dirty or satin petticoat dragging and she quickly turned around to look at the back of her dress to see if it was showing.

Shifting their attention to Griff, the two women batted their lashes and gazed at him as if he were a piece of Mrs. Bernard's freshly baked pie.

"Hello, Griffin," they said in unison, with coy smiles that made Grace want to yank their hair until they squealed.

"Afternoon," Griff replied, acknowledging the women and quickening his pace.

"Who are they?" Grace asked.

"Just some old acquaintances."

Grace looked over her shoulder and saw the two women huddled together, giggling as Reece nodded in her direction and tipped his hat. "They don't look that old to me," she said under her breath and followed Griff's lead to the picnic area.

Settling on a secluded spot next to a tree afforded Grace the opportunity to observe the rest of the picnic. It was a friendly group as far as she could tell. Certainly, they wouldn't all be like those women talking to Reece. Of course, some were speaking quietly to their companions, curious, she supposed, to see the girl Griff rescued in the hills but that was to be expected. There were just as many who called out to him and smiled warmly to her. She made eye contact with Rachel, who was waving wildly, in the crowd, and this set Grace at ease as she unpacked the picnic basket while Griff spread the blanket.

"I see you finally brought her out in public for the rest of us to meet."

A cowboy, who looked like a younger version of Griff, approached them and sat down. He ran his fingers through his sandy hair and flashed a playful grin as he inspected the plates full of food, carefully arranged in front of him. He reached for a piece of chicken but withdrew his hand when Griff slapped it away and grunted.

"You must be the pretty girl he's kept hidden on his ranch. Now that we've met, I can see why."

Griff crammed a fork stacked with food into his mouth not bothering to look up. "Grace, this is my baby brother Lance, who, as you can tell, is not so young that he can't get a licking from me if he doesn't behave. It should be apparent, now, why I haven't introduced him before."

"I don't recall that I was the one getting the licking when we were young," Lance said, reaching for the chicken again. "It's a pleasure to meet you ma'am. The entire family wanted to stop by and see how we could help but my brother, who has the manners of an old sow, said you were not feeling well enough for visitors. You look like you're feeling fine, now."

Griff picked up a biscuit and tossed it toward Lance then grabbed one for himself. "She's feeling better because she didn't have a house full of my relatives stumbling about, getting in the way. I told you when the time was right, everyone would have a chance to meet. Now that it's happened, it'll be up to Grace to decide if it was a good idea or not. Where's Matt and Elizabeth?"

I think it's a wonderful idea," said Grace. "Ever since I met Rachel I've wanted to get to know the rest of you. I've heard nothing but good things, so I'm pleased that you found us. Griff was right, though. I don't think I was prepared to see too many new faces while I was recovering. Especially when I couldn't remember old ones." She picked up an oblong pan and offered it to Lance. "Would you care for some cobbler?"

"No, thanks, but I'll have another piece of that chicken." Lance hesitated, looking at Griff who rolled his eyes and reluctantly nodded. He picked up a leg and tore off a piece. "Rachel had good words for you also, seeing how she's been the only one allowed on the premises. Pa is around here some place, anxious to say hello. I haven't seen Matt."

"Pa came too?" Griffin asked, putting down his fork and swallowing. "I'm surprised."

"As I said, he wanted to say hello. He was talking to Jesse the last time I saw him and sent me to tell you not to leave until you caught up with him."

"Tell him we'll be over as soon as we're finished eating"

Lance tossed the chicken bone on the plate and wiped his mouth. "Thanks for the meal. I'm heading over to the dance. Nice to finally meet you Grace." He grabbed another biscuit and stood up. "I'm sure we'll run into each other again before the night is over."

Grace watched as Lance walked away and caught sight of Reece encircled by a group of women fluttering around him like moths attracted to light and wondered if he shouldn't be attending to sheriff duties instead of entertaining the ladies.

They finished eating and headed toward a small gathering of men. Jesse smiled as they approached and giving her a hug, turned her to face the group.

"This is our little Gracie," he said with pride. "Grace these are some of the town folk you'll be getting to know."

He pointed to each man who nodded their head in acknowledgement as Jesse called out their name. "Henry Turner, long-time friend and ranch manager for Matt's wife before they were married. His sidekick Luke. Also worked for Elizabeth. Will Spencer, the finest gentleman this town has to offer, and the smartest. He and Margaret are close friends of the Kelly family. Jeb Miller, owns Miller Mercantile. You already met Juanita. Of course, Tom Kelly, can't forget the most important one of them all."

Grace blushed as she looked in the eyes of a large, gray haired man whose commanding presence over shadowed the rest of the men standing near him. He was nothing like Griff in looks or manner, although possessed the same dark eyes. She meekly said hello.

"It's about time my son let us get a gander at the woman he's been protecting. Jesse says Griffin is taking good care of you. Takes after his mother in that respect. Full of compassion. Why, when he was a boy..."

"Pa, for crying out loud." Flustered, Griff looked at Grace. "I'm sorry if my father is embarrassing you. "

"No, he's not. I think it's very nice that your father is interested in my wellbeing and he obviously thinks highly of you and your accomplishments. Isn't that correct, Mr. Kelly?"

"Well, of course," answered Tom a bit confused as to what he'd done wrong.

"Tom was just telling us about little Hope. Seems she's been under the weather." Jesse placed his hand on Griff's back, speaking softly. "You know your pa's just excited about seeing you and Grace."

"Matthew and his wife send their regrets. My little granddaughter has come down with a case of measles and Elizabeth will not budge from her side. They were disappointed they couldn't come. I plan to have you all over for a barbecue one of these days. It'll give you a chance to see the rest of the Emerald and time for us to get to know each other."

"That's a shame about your granddaughter, Mr. Kelly." Grace smiled at Griff. "And don't worry about Griffin taking good care of me. He's doing a wonderful job."

"We're going to head over to the dance now, if you will all excuse us."

"Don't forget that barbecue."

"I won't Mr. Kelly."

Griff pulled her from the men and strolled toward the area where the dance was ready to begin. As the evening grew dark, lanterns were placed on posts at the four corners of the area designated for dancing. The sides were lined with seating, where available, and a makeshift platform was built for the two fiddle players who were warming up. Tables with desserts and punch were set up on the side.

By this point, most families with young children had gone home. Occasionally, adolescent boys, who hadn't been dragged away by their parents, would run between chatting couples or swipe a piece of cake as they darted past the dessert table, only to feel the iron hand of Sheriff Cameron, who promptly thumped them on their nose and escorted them from the area. This part of the social was left to the grown-ups.

Grace saw Juanita Miller first. She was arranging chairs by the dance floor and she headed in that direction only to be stopped halfway there by Rachel and another woman in her mid-forties.

"Where have you been? Margaret and I thought you might have left." Rachel grabbed Grace's arms, smiling as she looked her over. "You look wonderful in that dress. I think I'd put it to shame now that I've seen it on you. I love your hair, don't you Margaret?"

"Griff and I were talking to your father," answered Grace. "I've been making my way over here slowly. I just now saw Mrs. Miller."

"This is Margaret Spencer. You've heard me speak of her."

Grace smiled demurely, at a loss for words after hearing so much about this woman who meant so much to the Kelly family. She was a tall, delicate woman with a warm smile. She possessed a caring touch as she took Grace's hand.

"I'm so glad you decided to stay for the dance. There are so many good people in this town who want to help if they can."

Grace thought she spoke in a soft though authoritative voice, as if she could organize a party or command an army with the same success. Margaret put her at ease immediately.

"Most of the ladies in town want an opportunity to show you we are civilized people, even in this wild state. We feel terrible that you were hurt, practically in our backyard, and hope you'll give us the opportunity to make it up to you however we can. I've planned a tea for the garden club whenever you feel up to it. I believe most of the members were afraid you might recover your memory and leave us before we've even had a chance to get to know one another. I must admit I'm a little jealous of Juanita Miller because she's already had the pleasure of spending time with you."

Grace smiled timidly. She was right, Margaret could plan a party, and if she showed up with a regiment of soldiers right now, Grace would not be surprised. "I promise I won't leave without having tea with your club."

"Well, I plan to hold you to that. Of course, Will and I want Griffin to bring you to dinner some evening. Let me introduce you to a few of the others before the evening gets away from us."

Margaret led Grace to a group of ladies who joined Mrs. Miller by the dessert table for a brief introduction, long awaited on their part. Edna Ferguson, wife of the bank president and mother of Rachel's present beau, Bart. Mary Bernard, owner of the local millinery and Mrs. Richter whose husband was the owner of the local mill and a business associate of Tom Kelly. Grace had to admit, Mrs. Richter didn't act that excited to meet her acquaintance and frowned when they were introduced.

They only had a few minutes before Griff led her away as couples lined up to form a square. They found a spot with the others as the music began. She didn't remember ever having danced and nervously apologized as she stepped on his feet. She saw the smug faces of the two young women she'd seen earlier with Reece and blushed with embarrassment, wondering if she might ever be able to attend another social again. Griff didn't seem to mind as he moved her around the dance floor practically swinging her out of the circle on one turn.

They danced through several songs and when the music finally stopped, she asked to take a break and sat with Rachel while Griff went to the dessert table to get some punch. Rachel was waiting for Bart Ferguson who had also made a trip to the dessert table and was standing in line with others who had the same idea.

Griff approached the table and scanned the desserts looking for one of Mary Bernard's pies. He always had room for one of her pies and tried to figure out how he could balance a piece and carry two glasses of punch at the same time.

Lance stood on the other side entertaining a couple of young ladies with one of his jokes and he glanced at Griff and grinned as the two women stood on each side of him, holding on to his arm. Griff laughed and shook his head, remembering the days when he was the one with girls clinging to each arm. Thank goodness, those days were past, he thought. Matt figured it out when he met Elizabeth. They were happy in their life and for the past two years Griff found himself wanting that same happiness. Even Reece had grown weary of it all.

One of the women pawing Lance let out a burst of laughter, clinging tighter to his arm. The sight of all this made Griff laugh too. He didn't begrudge Lance this time. He'd tire of it too when he got older.

"Griffin, where have you been?" A woman glided up behind him, sliding her arm through his, then maneuvered seductively closer. "I thought you would ask to bring me this evening. I've missed you."

"I've been busy Clara. I've got a ranch to run now and that doesn't leave much time for socializing," Griff tried to break free of the woman's grasp. "You should have come with someone else."

"Well, of course, I had plenty of invitations but I wouldn't think of going with anyone else but you. I know about that woman whose been staying at your ranch and I forgive you."

"I don't need any forgiveness, Clara. The only thing I've done is help a woman in trouble."

Grace was stunned as she watched Griff speaking to a woman who appeared to be making a scene as she threw herself at him. Others standing nearby were looking too and she was embarrassed for them both.

Rachel saw her expression and scooted her chair closer to Grace to avoid being over heard. "That's Clara Richter," she whispered. "I started to tell you about her yesterday. The girl doesn't give up."

"Who is Clara Richter?" Grace whispered back. "Didn't I just meet her mother?"

"Yes, and Clara is just like her. Worse maybe. She's crazy about Griffin. They courted at one time but Griff was never serious about her. Reece calls her Snooty Hooty." Rachel laughed loudly and looked around to see if anyone was paying attention to their conversation.

"Mr. Richter owns the mill and half interest in a silver mine with Pa. She thinks that entitles her to ownership of Griff and can't seem to get it through her head that he is not the least bit interested. She hangs on him every chance she gets."

Grace glanced over at Griff again. He was now backing up and wrestling with Clara to release her hold, smiling politely, glancing around at the staring audience as Clara chatted on. He looked to Lance, hoping his brother might rescue him from Clara's advances.

"Poor Griff," Rachel continued. "He's tried to break it off in a nice way but she just keeps throwing herself at him. Matt warned him that she was trouble and not to get involved with her. She's the only girl Reece and Griff have never fought over.

Grace was disappointed. Griffin had been so kind to her since he brought her to the Emerald. He made her feel special when they were together. Now it would seem as if she might not be special at all. Maybe, like Clara, his intensions were not serious and he would decide that she too was not the girl for him.

She sighed deeply and lowered her eyes, unable to watch anymore when a hand reached out to her. She looked up to find the friendly smile of Reece Cameron and was grateful to see him standing there.

"It's a beautiful evening and perfect for dancing. Will you do me the honor?"

"I'm not very good. There's a strong chance you'll end up regretting it." Grace looked over at Griff again and then back at Reece with apologetic eyes. "There's still time to change your mind."

Reece's strong arms lifted her off her chair then circled around her waist. "I have no intensions of changing my mind. It will be a pleasure."

He walked her to the dance floor, grinning as he drew her closer. Grace didn't know what to say and glanced back at Rachel who was staring in amazement.

The music started and they began to dance. She couldn't help smiling at him. The last time Reece held her in his arms she nearly shot him. He was attentive to her, unlike Griff who seemed to have found other company for the evening and her heart began to flutter with excitement. Reece saved her from humiliation and she was enjoying his company.

Finally, free of the clutches of Clara Richter, Griff turned back toward the seats, looking for Grace. He saw Rachel sitting there with Bart but Grace wasn't around and he began to worry until he spotted her on the dance floor, with Reece Cameron's arms wrapped around her.

I can't turn my back for a minute, he thought. Clara made another attempt at nuzzling close but he pushed her away in anger and she stormed off, followed by two other women.

Lance walked up and stood next to him watching Griff gnash his teeth. "What's wrong with you, it's just a friendly dance. You're making too much of it."

"You know it's more than that. Reece has had his eye on her from the beginning. He always wants what I have."

"Well it's not like you haven't wanted what he has, in the past. It's always been a game between you two and you've butted in as many times as he has. The only reason it bothers you now is because the stakes are higher this time. You're not doing a very good job of hiding your feelings. Heck, Clara Richter is the only one who can't see it and I believe even she is smart enough to notice."

Lance snickered and dropped his voice to a whisper. "Did you see her storm out of here. She's as mad as a hornet."

Griffin knew his brother was right about everything. He never cared before if Reece got the upper hand. He'd done the same thing but it was different now.

Lance picked up the punch glasses and handed them to Griff. "Leave it alone for tonight. It's been a good day. She's happy so don't spoil it. You can't blame Reece or any other man for showing interest. After the way Clara was carrying on, you need to worry about how Grace feels about you and not Reece."

Griff looked at Lance and knew he spoke the truth. He was sure Grace had seen Clara hanging on him. She wasn't aware that Clara meant nothing to him and that he does everything he can to avoid her. He couldn't blame Grace for being upset. He needed to explain the situation to her.

He pensively watched Grace and Reece on the dance floor. It was a sad day when his little brother was the voice of reason. He took the glasses and started to walk back to the seats then paused and turned around, looking at Lance. "Hey kid, if I've ever said anything mean to you, I meant every word of it."

Lance threw his head back, laughing out loud. "Me too, you old sow. Why don't you try kissing her? If that doesn't make her run then nothing will."

The dance ended but Reece stood in the circle waiting for the music to start again. Grace smiled nervously. She was enjoying the time she spent with him but wondered if she should go back and join Rachel. She was anxious to see if Griff had returned.

"Sheriff, I hate to interrupt but there's a couple of young fellas fighting over there. They're pretty liquored up and causing trouble," said a gentleman tapping Reece on the shoulder. "Someone's bound to get hurt."

Reece turned to Grace apologetically. "I'm afraid I'm going to have to take care of this. I'll be back as soon as I can." He walked off with the gentleman, leaving her to return to the seats and feeling relieved that she didn't have to make the decision about a second dance.

Drifting through the crowd, she heard the music start again and turned around hoping to catch Griff's attention as he stood with Lance. She hadn't gone far when the sound of rustling dresses and stomping feet caught her attention as three women paused behind her. She recognized two of the women from earlier in the day. They were talking with Reece when she and Griff arrived. The third woman had been clinging to Griff at the dessert table.

"She's nothing but a tramp," shouted the woman who was seen with Griff, earlier.

A couple standing by Grace turned around and stared as the woman spoke. "If she plans to steal Griff from me, she better think again. He has no interest in an unmarried woman shameful enough to live with two men. She has no respect."

"It's indecent," said the second woman. "She should be run out of town. She doesn't even have a proper dress. I heard Rachel tell someone she had to give that girl one of her own. Can you imagine?"

The couple next to Grace turned around again, frowning at the three women as they continued to speak in loud voices "Men don't marry loose women. Griff's father will never allow him to marry a woman like that."

"I heard Lance is positively mortified and has begged Griffin to kick her out at once."

"I heard Matt and Elizabeth didn't want to attend tonight because of her."

Grace had enough. Tears burned as they ran down her cheeks. The women were correct. She was a nameless, homeless nothing who had taken advantage of a kind-hearted man and embarrassed his family name. She couldn't bear to bring them more shame and wished Griff had left her in the hills to die. Everyone would have been better off. She couldn't listen any longer. Turning around, she pushed through the women, sobbing as she began to run. Grace didn't care where she went, as long as she got away from there and never saw Griffin Kelly again. She knew now she could never fit in.

Running through the trees, Grace saw the main road to town and was headed in that direction when a hand reached out and grabbed her arm, pulling her back with such force she almost fell to the ground. Looking up she saw the silhouettes of two men on horseback, their features hidden in the shadows. A third man stood holding tight to her arm. He smelled of sweat and beer as she struggled to get free. She cringed and began to shake as the man leaned forward, spraying saliva when he whispered in her ear.

"Well girlie, seems like you ain't as dead as we thought."

CHAPTER 9

SECRETS

Grace stood limp, head bowed, unable to bring herself to move from the spot where this odious man held her captive. She listened as his raspy voice echoed in her mind when he spoke and once again the memories of approaching horses bombarded her thoughts. "Please," she whimpered. "Please don't hurt me."

"Don't hurt you?" the man said, holding her arm so tight her fingers were tingling. "What's the matter, girlie? You think we're gonna hurt you? You know what we come for and why. We're not leaving without it. You turn everything over to me and we'll see about letting you live. If you give us anymore trouble then we're gonna all take a ride back up to them hills and you can do your beggin' there."

"I don't know what you want." Grace's shoulders shook as she stared at the ground, sobbing, afraid to look at the faces of the three men. "I don't know who you are. Please, let me go, I can't give you what you want if I don't know what it is you're looking for"

The man laughed out loud then reached with his free hand and slapped her so hard it took the breath out of her. Grace cried out in pain, touching her hand to her cheek. She desperately searched her mind for some clue as to who these men were.

"Don't know who we are?" said the man, his voice turning gruff again. He shook Grace so violently she lost her balance and fell to one knee. "I ain't stupid girlie and I ain't falling for that act you're putting on. You may have the sheriff and that starry-eyed boy fooled but I'm running out of patience. I ain't chased you clean across this state for you to tell me you don't remember who we are. Now you got something I want and I mean to get it. I don't care what I gotta do."

"But, I told you I don't have anything. I'll give you money if that's what you want."

The man lifted Grace to her feet and slapped her again. She cried out in pain, sobbing uncontrollably. "Money, you think I want money? You had your chance and money ain't gonna save your life now, girlie." He raised his hand to strike her.

"Pa, don't. There's no need to hurt her," one of the men from the shadows pleaded. "Anne, please give us what we want and I promise we'll let you go."

"Shut up, Lamont. You ain't promising anything. I've had my fill of this girl. You should have let me take care of this in those hills. I'm gonna end it right here."

He placed his hands around Grace's neck and slowly squeezed. Shots rang out from the distance and he paused, relaxing his grip. Shouting grew closer as the man watched people searching the fields by the dance area. The bobbing of lanterns moving in the direction of the road to town signaled he was running out of time.

"Lamont's right, Pa. It's not going to do any good to beat her to death. We need answers, first," said another voice hidden in the shadows. "Give her to me, we'll take her with us."

Voices grew closer. Grace could hear her name called as the once darkened field came alive with more and more lanterns dotting the grassy area like fireflies in the night. She knew if she didn't get away from these men they would kill her. They'd already tried it once in the hills.

More warning shots followed by someone yelling her name. It was Griff. Her pulse raced and tears of relief welled in her eyes. He'd come for her and she had to get to him before these vicious men carried her away.

She stomped down, grinding the heel of her shoe into the man's foot. His hands lay lose around her neck, and she grabbed his arms, pushing him with the whole strength of her body. He stumbled back in pain, cursing.

"Griff," she screamed as she ran toward the voices. "Griff, I'm here."

Griff yelled Grace's name and fired twice in the air as a signal to the others. He ran toward the road and the sound of Grace's voice.

"Pa, we gotta go, they'll be here any minute."

"I don't like leaving her," said the older man. "She knows too much even if she pretends she can't remember. I want to end this now." He pulled a gun from his holster, peering through the dark for his target.

"Forget it Pa," said a panicked voice. "We'll kill her later."

The three galloped from the protection of the trees to the main road, heading toward town. Grace ran to Griff, nearly knocking him over as she threw her arms around his neck, crying. "It was them," she murmured. "They were waiting for me."

"Did they hurt you? Why would you run off by yourself like that?"

"I don't know, I was upset and wasn't thinking clearly. I just needed to get away."

"You're safe now. That's the important thing."

"Well, looks like my plan worked." Reece walked to the spot where three horses stood minutes before. Standing with his hands on his hips, he looked down the road to town. "Unfortunately, we were in the wrong place to grab them. You alright, Grace? Doc Larson was behind me. He'll be along in a moment."

"I'm fine, now that it's over." Grace wiped her eyes and took Griff's hand as they joined Reece. The three stared down the dirt road, glittered with silver moonlight.

"Those guys have a lot of gall showing up like this. Half the town is here tonight," said Griff.

"I suspect they're desperate. Did they give you any hint as to what they wanted, Grace? I don't suppose they mentioned where they were heading or how we could find them?"

"They said quite a bit, actually, but it was mostly about how they wanted me dead." Grace's face puckered, tears running down her cheeks as she hid in the comfort of Griff's arms. "It was horrible." Her voice faded away as she remembered the raspy words of the older man when he threatened her.

"We've got to go after them, tonight. For her sake, we can't let them get away, this time." Griff eyed the men running across the field toward them and wondered if they could raise a posse at this hour. Many people had already left the social and those waiting behind were scared. Most men were concerned about getting their families home, safe. He glanced at Reece, dubiously. "It's obvious now, they're not going to stop until..."

"Griffin, what's going on?" Tom Kelly approached with gun drawn, followed by Jesse and the others. He paused for a moment to catch his breath. Bending forward, bracing himself with his hands stiffly clutching his thighs, he spoke in staggered spurts. "Were those the men? Is she safe?"

"Yes, Pa, it looks like they waited here in the trees for the right moment. Reece and I were just talking about mounting up and heading after them."

"Well, they picked the wrong crowd to tangle with. We've got enough men waiting and willing to go whenever you say the word. Where's Chet Larson? Did those scoundrels harm you, young lady?"

"I'm fine." The words were barely audible as she struggled to get them out. Her throat was dry making it difficult to speak. The accusations made by the men who briefly held her captive were astounding, and she was having trouble thinking of anything else.

She clung tightly to Griff. Her face stung from the slaps she suffered at the hands of the outlaw and her knee ached from falling to the ground, but none of that mattered now. She just wanted to go home.

"Grace is doing well, Pa," said Griff, trying to relax her hold around him. "Jesse can take her back to the ranch while we're gone. I guess Reece will want to make sure things are secure in town first. What do you think, Reece?"

The sheriff took a deep breath, pacing back and forth, still staring down the main road as he contemplated a plan for pursuing the men who tried to grab Grace and disrupt the church social. It's bad enough they wanted to hurt her, but he was especially put out with them for terrorizing his town. These people were his responsibility and as sheriff, he didn't take it lightly when thugs decided to ride in, threatening people. He wanted these men as badly as Griff but he was smart enough to know it would be a struggle."

"They've built up a big lead. They're half way to town by now, maybe farther if they know the back roads."

"They didn't have any trouble finding the social," said Griff.

"That's my point. It's dark and once we get into open country we'll have trouble following their trail. I've got the safety of these men to consider, as well as the horses." Reece looked at Grace, who peeked at him through Griff's arms. She knew what was coming and she grabbed his chest even tighter, burying her face again.

"This is going to be difficult at best, but I guess we've been in tighter spots. Let's mount up. We'll pick up Vance on our way through town. He's babysitting the jail for me tonight."

"No," Grace cried out as Griff freed himself from her arms. "Please don't go."

"I have to go, Grace. It's my duty to stand with these men who are willing to spend half the night searching for those vermin." Griff looked around the crowd of men who'd gathered. "Jesse will take you home. You'll be fine."

"Please, stay here with me, I don't want anyone to get hurt."

"No one is going to get hurt. Now, I need you to go home with Jesse," Griff said softly as he moved Grace toward his friend who stood huddled with the others.

"I'm crushed, Gracie," said Jesse, giving her a hug. "It stings my pride to have a pretty girl turn down an evening with me." He leaned close to her ear and whispered. "Don't you worry, they'll be home before you know it."

"Griff is staying here," said Reece.

"What are you talking about?" Griff searched the sheriff's face for an explanation. "I'm going along with the rest of you. Grace is just scared, but she'll feel better once Jesse gets her home."

"I'm afraid that won't work," replied Reece, shaking his head in disagreement. "You said yourself, these men had a lot of gall showing up here tonight with half the town at this social. Have you forgotten, they know where you live? Heck, they were in your backyard a couple of weeks ago and probably outside her window. What makes you think they won't show up again tonight or tomorrow? In fact, what makes you think they didn't go to the Emerald first and, not finding you home, came here? Maybe they've been watching your every move. We just can't take that chance anymore. You need to take Grace home."

Griff raised his hand in protest and started to interject but Reece stopped him.

"I know you think the right thing is to come with us and on any other occasion, I would agree. Deep down, you know you're better off staying at the ranch with Jesse in case of trouble. These men won't think twice about gunning her down and Jesse will have his hands full if they show up."

"He's right Griffin," said Tom. "No one here will think any less of you. We'd all stay if we were in your shoes. Besides, you've done the same for others in the past."

"I'm going with Reece," said Lance, stepping forward and standing next to the sheriff. "I can take your place with the posse."

"No, you and Jesse go back with Griff," Tom answered. "I agree with Reece. There's nothing to say those men won't be waiting to ambush you on the road or show up at the ranch later."

"Lance, you'll be more help to me and Jesse. We can use the extra gun." Griff stroked Grace's hair for a moment then gently touched his cheek to hers as he bent down to whisper in her ear. "I'm going to take you home where you'll be safe." She nodded then slowly released his neck.

"Tell Rachel to go back to town with Will and Margaret. She can stay there until we get back. With all of us gone, I don't want her staying by herself," said Tom as Griff took Grace's hand and turned back toward the crowd, still waiting at the dance area. "She'll kick up a fuss, but don't you give in to her."

Chet Larson examined Grace's injuries and, satisfied that she would not need any further medical attention, said goodnight. Griff watched the sheriff and his father lead the assembled men to their horses and slowly mount before galloping toward the main road with a thundering sound, kicking up dust in their wake.

Grace cringed as she and Griff approached the dance area. A couple of men were stacking chairs into the back of a wagon and she saw Juanita Miller wiping the dessert table with a damp cloth. It was humiliating to be led back to these people like a lost child. She thought again of the conversation between the women she'd overheard earlier and felt like a disgrace to Griff and his family.

She hoped to silently slip back to the carriage without having to speak with anyone but hadn't stepped a foot in that direction before Rachel reached out and hugged her. "I was so worried. I looked everywhere. One minute you were dancing with Reece and the next you disappeared. Then Griff started running toward the field calling your name and things seemed to explode after that. Men grabbing lanterns and shooting guns. It was terrifying."

"Rach, we don't need your theatrics right now. It's been a long evening."

"Theatrics," said Rachel with a disapproving eye as she strutted up to her brother, defiantly. "You're a fine one to talk. This wouldn't have happened if you stayed with her instead of talking to Clara all evening."

"All evening? I was gone for five minutes." Griff scanned the faces of the other women standing nearby. Most were garden club members who waited with Rachel during the search. Their inquisitive faces were intimidating and his face reddened as he felt their scorn. He moved closer to his sister and whispered through gritted teeth.

"You know that woman is crazy. I tried to get away from her but she's like an annoying fly that keeps buzzing around. Anyway, I left Grace with you so if you hadn't let her run off with Reece she'd still be sitting in that chair safe and sound. What were you doing while I was gone?"

"You were gone longer than five minutes and Clara as usual was making a spectacle of herself, falling all over you. It was nauseating. You could have tried a little harder to get away. Poor Grace had to watch the whole thing."

Lance shimmied over and stuck his face between those of his two siblings. "I can't believe you two picked this time to go at each other," he grumbled. "We've got more important things to do. Like getting home without being shot. Now, let's get packed up and go. Oh, and Rachel, Pa says you're to go home with the Spencers and no arguments over it."

"I believe all of you need to behave. You're acting like spoiled children and your father would be ashamed to see you carry on like this in front of all these people."

Margaret Spencer stood stoically with her arms crossed, frowning as the three momentarily stared, then dropped their eyes, awaiting her explanation of the meaning of propriety. She paused as if allowing them to squirm a little before speaking again.

"Rachel dear, it's been an exciting evening and one we shall long remember, but your brother is very concerned for Grace's safety as well as your own. This is not the time to trouble him with your opinion of his attentions toward certain young ladies or to doubt his loyalties to your new friend. Now, your father has left instructions for you to stay with us so I suggest you locate your young man and have him take you to our house. I believe he is helping Will load the dessert table on to the wagon."

Rachel glared at Griff before putting on her best pouty face and strode in the direction of the wagon, looking for Bart. Margaret turned her attention to Griff who flashed a sheepish grin, hoping to deflect her displeasure. Lance stepped behind his brother as if that would shield him from her sharp words.

"Griffin, I'm disappointed at the display of impatience with your sister, who, like you, is worried about Grace's safety. Rachel is a wonderful, loving, young lady who cares very deeply for those she feels close to as well as those she loves. I'm confident the two of you will apologize for arguing and saying things neither of you meant. In the meantime, Will has already spoken to Horatio Ferguson and they plan to follow you back to the ranch as extra protection. Edna has already left with Mary Bernard and Bart has agreed to see that Rachel and I get home safely, as well."

"Margaret, this is asking a lot of Will and Mr. Ferguson. I appreciate the offer, but I feel like we have dragged so many people into this mess already."

"Nonsense. you know you're like family to us and we won't be persuaded from these plans." She hugged Griff and kissed his cheek. "You know we all love you. Tell Rachel you're sorry when you get a chance," she whispered. "You'll feel better."

"Yes, ma'am."

Margaret turned with a casual grace and headed across the dance floor where Bart and Rachel were waiting. As Griff watched them climb into Bart's buggy, a slow smile spread over his face. Margaret possessed a talent for gently putting people in their place when they strayed. Although her words could be piercing, he felt he was a better person because of her guidance.

"Well," he said turning to Lance. "We might as well head home. You think we ought to take the usual road or try the back way? If they're waiting for us, we might have a chance to bypass them by staying off the main path."

"I vote for the back way but it's whatever you think is best."

"We'll see what the others say but the back road is my choice."

No one spoke on the ride home. Grace sat silently, reviewing every detail of those horrifying moments when she faced the three men. She had no idea what they were looking for and no idea how she could make herself remember. It sickened her to think of the trouble she had caused.

Her escort of men listened to every rustling leaf, snapping twig and scurrying animal as the trotting horses pulled the surrey which seemed to jump and bounce on every curve of the old dirt road leading to the ranch. It was seldom used since the new thoroughfare had been carved through the county as a connecting route for the stage running from Denver to Carson City and west to California. The old back way was overgrown with grass making it difficult to see in the dark.

Griff stared straight ahead, his pistol in his lap, flinching when the horses seemed spooked. The others were staggered strategically by the carriage with hands on their guns, glancing nervously around. Lance and Will Spencer on the left, Jesse and Horatio Ferguson on the right. When the carriage passed the gate, the party came to a halt. Griff and Lance searched the house before allowing Grace to enter. Jesse and the others checked the surrounding buildings and, satisfied that nothing suspicious had taken place, Will and Horatio bid them goodbye and disappeared into the night.

Everyone was exhausted but as they climbed the porch steps, Griff knew no one was ready for sleep. Lance and Jesse took care of the horses while Griff made coffee and set out the last pieces of chicken and cobbler left from the picnic. Grace pulled the combs from her hair and threw them on the table as her brown locks tumbled down around her shoulders. She looked at the beautiful dress, borrowed from Rachel, which now carried stains and a layer of dust. How could she ever repay her friend, she wondered?

She could still smell the stench from the three outlaws and headed for the bath to wash off the dirty feeling that lingered as the others sat down to eat. When she emerged again she joined the three men in the front room. Lance had retrieved the bottle of bourbon Griff kept stored in a cabinet and was pouring a glass for the three when Grace sat down. He filled a fourth glass and set it on the table pushing it toward her. She looked at Griff not knowing what to do.

"A little won't hurt," he said as he picked up the glass and handed it to her. "It will make you sleep better."

She took a sip and made a sour face as the whiskey burned her throat. She knew the three men would want to hear the details of her encounter and had no idea where to begin. The men waited as she took another sip, allowing some time to collect her thoughts before speaking.

"They called me Anne. Well, at least one of them did. They say I have something they want but I have no idea what it is."

"Your name is Anne?" Griff sat up with interest and took her hand, smiling.

"I once knew a gal in Wichita by the name of Anne. Pretty redhead as I remember." Jesse sent a devilish wink toward Lance who scowled back. He cleared his throat and took another drink, waiting for Grace to continue.

"No last name," she said with a nervous smile. "But I guess it's a start."

"It's a pretty name," Griff said, trying to ease the tension she was feeling. "And a pleasant start. What else did they say?"

"Well, I can't say any part of it was pleasant but you're right, it is a good start. I admit much of it is blurry. I was so frightened and sure they would kill me, it's difficult to remember everything. I racked my brain on the way home trying to recall as much as I could."

"Do the best you can Gracie. We understand."

"I could only see the face of the man who was holding my arm. The other two were hidden in the shadows, but I recognized their voices. The older man is their father and he called one of them Lamont."

Do you know someone named Lamont? Is any of that familiar?" Lance asked.

"No, but he was nicer than the others. I could tell, he really didn't want to hurt me."

"They tried to kill you. How on earth can you think he was nice?" Griff was agitated at her choice of words. Nothing about these men was nice.

This time it was Jesse who scowled as he motioned for Griff to sit back and keep quiet. Lance refilled the glasses, handing one back to Grace. "Why would you say Lamont was nice?" he asked with a sympathetic smile.

"Well," Grace hesitated, looking at Griff as she spoke. "The older man was hitting me and Lamont told him to stop. He said they would let me go if I gave them what they wanted. That wretch of a man kept slapping me, demanding an answer but everyone I gave would not satisfy him."

Griff cupped her chin with his hand and raised her head slightly so he could inspect her bruised face. His desire to catch and punish these men became stronger. "What did Doc Larson say?"

"That I would heal." Grace delicately wiped her cheek with her fingers. "That this would all be gone in a couple of days."

"Grace, I swear I'm going to track these men down and make them pay. You will never have to be scared again." He clenched his fists and for a moment, wished he hadn't let Reece talk him out of going with the posse.

Jesse reached out and touched Griffin's shoulder trying to keep him calm. He could see the young man's anguish and searched for a way to lessen his guilt as they listened to Grace's story.

"What about their faces, Gracie? Was the cowboy who appeared outside Miller's among them?"

"I don't know, Jesse. I already told you I couldn't see their faces but I've met them before, I'm sure of it. There was a familiarity with the way they talked to me. As if they were a large part of my past. I may not be able to recognize them but I can remember their voices and I've heard all of them before.

The old man was rough and called me girlie just like in my dreams. It made my skin crawl but I won't forget what he looked like. The younger one, named Lamont, had a kind voice. I'm convinced he meant me no harm. I wish I knew what they wanted so I could give it to them and they would leave me alone."

"It could be anything, although none of the contents in the saddle bag seem valuable," Griff said. "Unless it was that beaded purse. Maybe those are real jewels."

Jesse shot a skeptical glance at Griff. "What about the horse? She's of good stock. She'd catch a fair price."

"They had their chance in Carson City. If they wanted her bad enough, they would have taken her from the gentleman who bought her without thinking twice. Reece has had that horse attached to every hitching post in town almost begging them to take her. Besides, the filly isn't worth killing for. Not unless she has solid gold teeth."

"Maybe it's the saddle," said Lance. "I can't see it being worth losing a life over."

"What would be worth killing for?" Grace asked.

"I don't know. It's different for each person I suppose. Cattle maybe, or land," Griff answered.

"Water rights if there's a drought," Lance added. "Remember Pa telling us about those ranchers in Texas?"

"These men didn't look like they owned a clean shirt. I can't imagine they own land," Grace said.

"Gold or silver," said Lance. "Maybe she owns a gold mine in the hills."

"Maybe your head isn't screwed on tight," said Griff.

"Hey, it's just a thought and no worse than a hand bag made of real jewels," laughed Lance. "It's all conjecture at this point."

"Well, I don't suppose we're gonna find out until we catch up with these scoundrels," Jesse said as he yawned and put down his glass. "I don't know about the rest of you but if I'm going to be worth anything tomorrow, then I'm going to need my beauty sleep, tonight. I say we call it a day and think on this some more tomorrow."

"Lance can sleep in the store room at the back of the house. Jesse, you and I will sleep out here. I think it's better if we all stick together."

He took Grace's hand and led her to the bedroom door, lingering before she entered. "I'm sorry I let you down. I was supposed to protect you but I wasn't there when you needed me."

"You aren't to blame. It's my fault. I was foolish to leave the dance and I don't blame you for being angry. I'll understand if you want me to leave. I know I've been an embarrassment to you."

"Embarrassment?" Griffin replied. "I don't want you to leave. Who put that idea into your mind?"

Grace was hesitant to answer. It seemed silly now that she had paid attention to the ramblings of Clara and her friends. She hesitated, too ashamed to explain.

"Grace," Griff said finally. "We both have to learn to trust each other if we're going to make it through this. We can't keep secrets. I want to know why you ran away."

She took a deep breath and repeated the remarks made by Clara and the other women. Griff shook his head in disgust as he listened then told her about his brief courtship, apologizing for not warning her about Clara.

"She's spoiled and possessive when she has no right. I should have known that seeing you would bring out the worst. No one in town considers it improper for you to stay here. They understand you were injured and that you would be lost without our help. I think tonight proved that. Our friends understand it is essential for you to have our protection and if someone doesn't like it then they will have to contend with the entire Kelly clan. However," he hesitated for a moment as he took her hand. "If you feel more comfortable somewhere else, I'm sure Rachel would love for you to stay with her and Pa."

"No, I don't want that," Grace answered loudly. "I mean... I certainly appreciate the offer to stay with your family and it would be nice to talk with Rachel more but I think it's best to stay here. You know...I'm sure it's safer with you and Jesse and well...I don't want to leave."

Griff touched her hand to his lips, kissing it softly. She gazed at him then whispered his name. He pulled her toward him and kissed her, lingering just a moment, listening to her breathe and soaking in the sweet smell of lavender. "Get some sleep," he said smiling as she walked into the bedroom and closed the door.

Griff sank deep into the leather chair. Turning down the lamp, he peered into the darkness, wondering where Reece and the others were at that moment. His friend was smart and a good lawman. If those men were to be found, the sheriff would be the one to do it. He closed his eyes, wishing the nightmare was over for all of them and hoping for a chance to show Grace a life without fear, or secrets, where she would be loved.

CHAPTER 10

UNDER THE MOON

"You remember, don't you Anne?"

The boy was fourteen with a look of forlorn in his dark eyes as his outstretched hand held three red roses. He stood in the tall grass of the pasture, wearing worn pants and a frayed shirt, beckoning her to come closer. "Where did you hide it? Give us what we want."

"It's under the moon," Grace replied, backing away from the boy. "Can you see it under the moon?"

Dressed in a nightgown, she floated toward the black filly, standing by the stream. Her leather bag, its rose emblem etched on the side, hung from the saddle. It was hot and the sun's rays beat down on her forehead wrapped in a bloody cloth.

"Find it or we'll kill you like we killed your pa. Where is the moon, Anne?" The boy inched closer, reaching out with menacing hands curling around her neck.

"I don't know, Lamont," Grace cried. "Run, they're coming." She tried to get away from the boy but her feet would not move. Her blood-splattered boots stuck firmly to the ground as she struggled to get away.

"Find the moon, Anne," the boy called. "Find the moon."

Grace sat up in bed, gasping for air. The room was still dark, and she sat in the stillness, listening, half expecting to see the boy in his ragged clothes standing nearby. Dangling her feet from the side of the bed, she wiped the beads of perspiration from her forehead with shaking hands, her heart pounding.

"Well, that was a wild one," she muttered, looking around for her robe. She poured cold water into a basin, splashed her face, then stood for a moment, looking in the tiny mirror, replaying the dream in her mind.

"Find the moon, Anne," she said to her reflection. "He wants you to find the moon." She closed her eyes and sniffed the air, slowing exhaling. "Coffee. Griff must be up."

Grace ran a brush through her tangled hair, her eyes watering as the bristles tore at the knotted ends. It was so beautiful last night, she thought, and now it looked like a worn-out mop head. She dropped the brush and, dividing her long locks into three sections, began to braid them. Thoughts of Griff and the kiss they shared filled her mind and she giggled to herself wishing they hadn't had Jesse as an audience. She would have preferred their first kiss to come with a little more romance. A moonlight stroll, hand in hand, as he escorted her home, Griff would have paused to gaze into her eyes to tell her how wonderful she was, then taken her into his arms, professing his love, before kissing her longingly. They certainly had a stroll in the moon light. Only in their case, they only paused long enough to wave goodbye to a posse of men riding out to hunt down a band of criminals. Grace giggled again as she tightened the belt on her robe and crossed the room. She didn't care how that first kiss came about. Only that it happened. Maybe Griff did think more of her than Clara Richter, after all. The evening certainly wasn't perfect but it was still a success, despite the arrival of those men.

The front room was quiet when she opened the door. Blankets lay on the chair, neatly folded with pillows piled on top. The muffled sound of conversation coming from the kitchen caught Grace's attention and she shuffled in to find Jesse and Griff sitting in their usual spots at the table.

"How'd you sleep?" Griff rose, grinning, as she crossed the room. The memory of last night's kiss was still on his mind as he boyishly stood at attention, watching her demurely cross the room. "Want some coffee?"

"Yes, thank you." Grace glanced at Jesse then back at Griff and blushed. "I didn't hear you two get up. I have to admit, I was so exhausted, I wouldn't have heard a thing, Where's Lance?"

"Still asleep," Jesse answered. "That boy is not known as an early riser. I think Griff is going to have to drag him out of bed soon. We've got chores to do and Griff wants him to go into town."

"So, no nightmares last night?" Griff said with a hopeful look. "No regrets?"

"No, regrets," smiled Grace, shyly. "And, I wouldn't call what I experienced a nightmare. More of an enlightening dream. A little scary but one that could trigger memories if I'm lucky. I think one of those men who grabbed me was part of it, only he was a boy. I believe they killed my father"

Griff and Jesse looked at each other and then at Grace. There was an awkward silence, neither knowing what to say as they waited for her to go on. Jesse cleared his throat and fidgeted with his coffee cup, glumly soaking in each word while Griff stared with mournful eyes, unsure of how to respond.

"I must have known the one named Lamont when we were younger and that's why he was a boy in my dream. We might have been friends. He told me they killed my father and I confessed that whatever they want is someplace under the moon."

"Grace, it's just a dream. It doesn't mean your father is really gone," said Griff. He squeezed her hand gently, "Lots of crazy things happen in dreams that aren't true."

"I realize that, but something inside me says this is real. It makes sense if you think about it. You know, why no one has ever come looking for me. He called me Anne, just like last night and then he said they would kill me like they did my pa. I believe it's all true."

"It sounds like a mixed-up batch of jambalaya to me," said Jesse. He suddenly threw up his hands in exasperation. "What moon? Everything's under the dang moon. That doesn't tell us anything. And don't you go thinking there's no one out there looking for you, either. You got plenty of people worrying."

"It's a dream, Jesse. They seldom make sense. It's good that she's recovering memories, even if they're cryptic messages from some boy named Lamont. Yes, they're vague, but every bit gets us closer to the truth."

"Well, maybe you're supposed to look for this thing when it's dark. You know, when you would be under the moon." Jesse shook his head, grumbling. "Don't know how you could find anything in the dark. Sounds like a good way to break your neck, stumbling around."

"I'm sure there's more to it than that, Jesse," replied Griff, grinning as he imagined scads of people walking aimlessly around in the night, tripping over each other in search of an unknown object."

"Well, you can count me out," said Jesse with a grunt.

"Are you sure about your father?" Griff asked, turning to Grace.

"Yes, I believe these dreams are the way I process truths from my past. Truths I can't seem to bring myself to remember any other way. As if they are too painful to think of when I'm awake, so they sneak their way in to my mind when I'm sleeping. Not all at once. Just a little at a time so they won't be too overwhelming. I don't understand it either, but my father is dead and whether in the dark of night or midday sun, whatever those men want is under a moon. Any news from Reece and your pa?"

"Nothing," Griff said. "That's why I want Lance to go to town. I'm hoping someone has heard from them and he'll need to stop by the Spencer's to check on Rachel. They'll be wanting to know how we fared through the night."

"Stick close to the house today, Gracie, until we hear something," Jesse said. "I'm going out to take a look at that buggy. I want to make sure we didn't rattle the wheels off on that ride home last night. I'd hate to send it back to Tom, damaged."

"We'll have to start calling her Anne, Jesse."

"Maybe so but she'll always be Gracie to me." Jesse gave her a hug and started for the door.

"There was a time when I didn't have a single name and now I have two. I'd like to stick with Grace for now, until I discover who Anne really is."

"Well then, Grace. I think I'll go wake up my little brother before the morning is over. You relax for a while." Griffin squeezed Grace's hand again. "I'm sure we'll hear some news soon."

Grace sat at the table alone, thinking about the words from the boy in her dream. If he were to be believed, her father was gone. Gunned down, maybe, and left for dead as she had been? What about the rest of her family? She continued to be tormented by these questions.

There was an air of anticipation as they waited to hear from the sheriff. The morning slipped away into afternoon and still no word. Grace could tell that Griff and Jesse were having a difficult time focusing on their work. They would pause frequently and look toward the road in anticipation of seeing Lance appear and when he did not, they resumed their tasks, saying very little in the process.

Grace took advantage of her free time and finally looked through Griff's collection of books stored in the spare room at the back of the house. She cleaned them weekly but had never taken the time to pull one out of the bookcase and open the cover. There was plenty of Dickens, a couple by Melville and a group of old dime novels stacked together. She lifted one of the thin magazines from the pile and laughed. *Seth Jones and the Captives of the Frontier.* Certainly, an exciting western adventure for a boy growing up in Nevada.

Perusing the rest of the titles she decided on a novel entitled *Woman in White.* It was a mystery and a topic Grace felt appropriate considering her present situation. Sitting in the comfortable leather chair, she began to read but, interesting as the story was, she found herself pausing at times to gaze down the path toward the road or glancing at the clock on the mantle.

Lunch came and went before Lance returned in late afternoon, riding the black filly. Climbing the steps of the porch he laid a dark leather saddle down and handed an envelope to Griff.

"Everything all right in town?" Griff said when he noticed the unsettled look on his brother's face.

"The Spencers are good. Will and Mr. Ferguson made it home with no problems. They're keeping Rachel busy although she asked me to bring her here. I told her no, of course."

"What about the rest?" Griffin asked.

Lance looked with furrowed brow but did not say a word. He glanced toward the road and back at Griff.

"I can read your face, Lance," Griff said, fearing the worst. "Let's go inside and sit down. You want something to eat?"

"No, Thanks. Margaret took care of me. I picked up the saddle at Reece's office. The stationmaster at the depot said it came this morning from Denver along with that letter from the sheriff." Lance pointed to the envelope Griff was holding. "You better read it."

Griff pulled back the flap of the envelop and pulled out several pages. The first was a letter which he read, then passed over to Jesse. The second, larger paper contained a sketch of a man in his fifties. His round face dotted with pock marks showing through a white stubby beard. The word *Wanted* in bold letters was printed above. Grace looked at the drawing and grabbed her throat as if unable to breath, her mouth opened in a silent cry. The color drained from her face. She was light headed as she fell against Griff's shoulder.

"Everything is going to be alright," Griff said softly, trying to soothe her fear. "Jesse's going to get you some water. Is this one of the men who hurt you?" She nodded yes and took a sip from the glass, gradually regaining her composure.

"It's the man who called me girlie. The older man."

Jesse picked up the poster and read aloud to the others, pausing after each sentence, conscious of Grace's reaction. "Wanted, for murder and cattle rustling in Colorado and Utah. Luther Bannister and his sons, Lamont and Luke. Three thousand dollars reward offered. He looked up at the other three as he tossed the notice aside. "Dead or alive."

Grace tried to ignore the face printed on the poster as it lay on the table staring back at her. It was treacherous and a reminder of everything ugly that had happened. She turned her attention to Griff as he read the letter from the Denver sheriff but caught herself peering down at the hateful eyes of the man who wanted her dead. Shivers ran down her spine at the thought of last night's encounter and she closed her eyes as if that would make the memory go away.

"These men have been wanted for a long time," Griff said. "They've been running cattle for years. Stealing small numbers from different ranches so no one gets suspicious. Fewer cattle make it easier to hide their operation. Most of the ranchers around here have been losing a few at a time, me included, so the consensus was that

Indians were cutting them out of the herd or they strayed off and were killed by animals. It's why I was up in the hills the day I found you, Grace. Indians haven't been a problem for years. I thought it might be a cougar. We might not have figured it out if these Banisters hadn't shown up looking for you. The letter says the cattle are moved out of the area, maybe even out of state and usually held on a ranch owned by a dishonest cattle broker. The brands are altered, making it difficult to detect the theft, then the broker either sells them to a group who will drive them to market or has his own men take care of it. The cattle broker pays off the rustlers, makes big profits, and sits back while everyone else does the work. If things get too hot, he packs up, leaves town and starts up again somewhere else. The sheriff says he's thankful we contacted him and he's willing to help in catching the Bannisters."

"Well, at least we know their story," said Jesse. "I guess it's about what we figured. Of course, we still don't know where Gracie fits into all of this."

"There's something else," Lance said as Griff folded the letter. "Reece, Pa and the others haven't returned."

"Well, that's not surprising," said Griff. "You know Reece isn't about to give up easily. This won't be the first time he drags a posse around for days, chasing a criminal. Why does that surprise you?"

"When I stopped by the Spencer's, Will had some news. Information he was keeping from Margaret and Rachel." Lance ran his fingers through his hair and took a deep breath.

Grace glanced at Griff who sat silently, studying the troubled face of his brother. "Go on, it's not doing any good to keep it to yourself. What did Will say?"

Lance ran his hand through his hair again and somberly looked at Griff. "One of Reece's men came riding into town not long before I got there. He was looking for Doc Larson. The deputy said the posse followed the Bannisters all night, up through the hills where they found a camp site. Of course, the Bannisters weren't there. Reece picked up their trail heading west. According to the deputy, the posse has them pinned down in a rugged area about twelve miles from here, hiding in a bunch of cliffs or something. Gun fire going on all morning. Men are hurt and they've called for the doc."

"Who's been hurt?"

"Will doesn't know. The deputy who rode in was in bad shape, himself. Doc Larson patched him up and they both headed back to those cliffs to help the others."

Griff looked at Jesse and slowly rose. He grabbed his hat hanging from the peg by the front door and glanced at Grace.

"Go on, she'll be safe with me. You boys be careful. Those Bannisters are a mean bunch. It'll be difficult to bring them down."

"Get the rifles from the back room, Lance. I'll saddle the horses." Griff headed for the front door. "Grace, we got any of those biscuits left from breakfast? You might as well pack that ham too. There's sure to be some hungry men when we get there."

"No, please don't go. I can't bear the thought of you getting hurt." Grace ran to Griff, throwing her arms around him as if her strength might keep him from leaving the house.

"I have to go. I know you're scared but I can't stay here anymore while the others are out there. This is my fight and I'm not staying home."

"It's my fight," said Grace, as tears began to trickle down her cheeks. "I should be the one going."

Griff leaned forward and gently kissed her, holding on for a moment as she softly cried on his shoulder. "I have to go. I'll never forgive myself if I don't. Jesse will stay with you until I get back." He turned and walked out the door toward the barn.

Lance carried the rifles from the back room and down the front porch steps stopping by Grace who stood clutching the railing as tears ran down her cheeks. "I know you're hurting and he is too."

"What?" Grace turned when she realized Lance was standing there.

"It's not easy for him to leave, but he's got that ache in his gut. The one a man gets when he knows his life will never be right until he sets things on a straight course. Let him finish this. I'll make sure he sends word, if he can. You just make sure you've got some of that blackberry cobbler waiting for us when we get back."

"I will." Grace watched him shove a rifle in the scabbard of each horse. "You're a good brother."

"Yeah," said Lance as he ran his fingers through his wavy hair and smiled slyly. "That's what they tell me."

She placed the burlap pouch of food into Griff's saddle bag trying to smile as Griff hugged her then slowly unwrapped her arms from around his neck and mounted Rascal.

"Keep each other safe," she said, her voice cracking as she spoke.

"We always have."

She waited until they reached the road before turning to Jesse, sobbing hysterically. "This is all my fault. I should never have gotten him involved. Now I've put his entire family in danger. His father, brother, even Rachel isn't allowed to stay by herself for fear she may be hurt."

"This is not your fault. Those outlaws are to blame. You listen here, little miss. It's going to take more than a few scoundrels to stop that young man. He's got the Kelly fire in his eyes and he will not quit until these men are caught and punished."

"That's what Lance said. He called it an ache in his gut."

"Lance is a smart lad. Wise for his young years, but he's right and Griff is going to need a strong woman waiting for him when he gets back. Now, you and I are going to eat a little supper. We'll need to save some because those boys will be hungry when they return, which will be in no time at all. In the meantime, you can tell me about this book you've been reading. Must be a good one."

Grace was in a daze as she walked through the motions of preparing supper. She could think of nothing else but the posse perched in unknown cliffs, engaged in a gun fight with a group of men called Bannister. Try as she may, the name meant nothing to her and it should. Jesse was right. They had finally revealed the identity of her attackers and yet, there was nothing in the discovery that pointed to her role in their lives. She could be just as guilty as them.

Few words were spoken as she and Jesse sat at the table. She could not bring herself to eat and even Jesse seemed to have lost his appetite. As instructed, extra food was prepared and stored away carefully for Lance and Griff. Jesse put her saddle in the barn and secured the buildings before they settled in for the evening.

She rambled on as long as possible, telling Jesse the story of *The Woman in White* as they sat by the fire. When she ran out of things to say, she tried reading the book instead, looking up with every sound, forced to start over after each pause. They finally decided on a game of checkers, something Grace did not enjoy, even in happy times. She went through the motions of moving the pieces around the board in haphazard fashion while Jesse, very pleased with his game strategy, jumped from square to square gathering pieces. The clock on the mantel moved slowly as the evening dragged on and there were times when Grace was sure she would lose her mind if Griff did not return soon.

Having given up on checkers, the two sat quietly, deep in their own thoughts, when Jesse rose and walked to the window and peered out. He could see the shadows of horses slowly approaching from the road and picked up the gun lying on the table.

"Grace, I want you to go in the bedroom and lock the door." "What is it, Jesse," she said, suddenly turning pale.

There's men heading to the house from the road and since I'm not sure who they are, I think it's best if you stay in the other room until I figure out what they want."

"Is it Griff?" Grace ran to the window to watch the horses as they drew closer, with the hope he was finally home."

"Maybe and maybe not. They're moving awfully slow. That's why it's best if you go to the bedroom. Don't light the lamp and make sure you sit clear of the window." He cocked the gun as he stared at the approaching riders. "I wish Griff hadn't taken both of those rifles. Go on, Gracie."

She did as Jesse asked and sat on the floor, motionless in the dark, listening to the slow steps of horses as they reached the house. The front door opened and muffled sounds of men shuffling in could be heard as she waited. Then a familiar voice called her name. Unlocking the door, she flung it open and into the arms of Griff. Nestled in his chest, Griff held her tight, then released her and turned toward Jesse who was helping Reece to walk as they slowly crossed the floor and into a chair.

"Reece," she gasped when she saw the bloody bandage wrapped around his chest. "You're hurt." She lightly touched the oozing wound causing him to moan, then turned to Griff. "What happened? What should I do to help?"

"Put on a pot of coffee," Jesse said. "And set out that food you saved. I imagine these men are hungry. Break out the bourbon, Griff. It might be the best thing for him right now."

Grace ran to the kitchen to prepare the food while Griff filled three glasses. Reece laid back against the sofa, groaning softly and wincing as he tried to slow his rapid breathing. He took the glass with a shaking hand and downed it in one gulp. Griff refilled the glass as Jesse fetched a pillow leaning the sheriff forward long enough to place it gently behind his back. He spread a blanket over him but Reece threw it aside.

"I don't need that," he grumbled. "I'll take another glass of that whiskey, though.

Grace brought out plates of food for the men with the promise of coffee to follow. She sat beside Reece, wiping his forehead with a damp cloth and picking at his wound. "Does he need clean bandages? This looks like it will get infected it we aren't careful. I've got some in the other room."

"Leave him be for now," said Griff, pulling her hand away. "Let him rest a bit before you start mothering him. Jesse will change those bandages later. That hole he's got in his side is a gruesome sight."

Reece finished a second glass of whiskey and grimaced as he began to speak in broken sentences with labored breath. "It was just as we thought. Tracking was difficult but we picked up their trail north of town and followed it up through the hills. It was obvious they'd been holed up for days, waiting for the right time. I think that little filly must have done her job in catching their attention. They had moved on by the time we discovered where they'd camped but found their tracks again, heading west, so kept going."

Grace held a plate under his chin, spooning in bites between sentences. Reece glanced at Griff with a sly grin and laid his head on her shoulder for a minute before taking another spoonful of food.

"I think it's best to keep your head up." Griff glared back at his friend. "Don't want you choking on those potatoes." Grace gave him a sideways look of disapproval then gently wiped Reece's face again.

Reece held up the glass, half full of bourbon. "Doc Larson gave me something for this pain but it's not working as well as I'd like. Seems, this remedy is doing a better job." He poured the remaining bourbon into his cup of coffee and continued.

"We finally found them in some cliffs above a stream over in the next county. Jesse, do you remember when Griff and me and Matt went hunting over by Sweetwater when we were younger and ended up camping in a grove of trees near some cliffs?"

"I remember Tom being worried about letting you three go off by yourselves for a couple of days and I remember that you and Griffin probably bickered the whole time," Jesse replied.

"They're the same cliffs, where Elizabeth was taken. Remember that gambler from a couple of years ago?"

"The one after the race horse?" Jesse asked.

"Yeah, that's the one," said Reece. "What was the name of that guy?"

"No one cares, about the gambler, now." Griff could tell the whiskey was getting the best of his friend, causing him to lose his train of thought. He reached for the cup Reece was holding but Reece pulled it away. "We all remember you were the only one who got a deer on that trip and you've never let anyone forget it. Finish telling them the story."

"Well, these guys were dug into those cliffs so they had the high ground and we couldn't tell exactly where they were. We decided to wait until morning to flush them out. They started shooting as soon as the sun came up. Caught Vance in the leg first thing. I killed one before I was hit. After Tom got hurt, I sent back to town for Chet Larson. There was a moment when I didn't think some of us were going to make it out of there. Doc said the bullet that hit me went clean through."

"Mr. Kelly was shot too?" Grace shouted.

"Shot in the thigh. The whole thing just made him mad. You know, that Kelly pride. Doc Larson had the wound wrapped petty tight to stop the bleeding until they could get him back to the ranch and remove the bullet. Lance is there with him now and they sent for Griff's brother, Matt. Will Spencer is taking Rachel home to help."

"Don't worry, my father is too stubborn to die," said Griff with a grin. "He'll be up and around tomorrow, knowing him."

"How many of those outlaws were left by the time Griff and Lance got to the cliffs?" Jesse asked.

"Two," Griff replied "And they were not about to give up. Like Reece said, they had the advantage of the high ground. For a while, it looked like they might just pick us off, one at a time. With Pa, Reece and Deputy Vance hurt, it was up to me and Lance and the rest of the men to move as far up the cliff as we could, trying to get the best shot. Once the second man went down, the third one moved even higher and farther into the crevice of the rocks."

"He was smart, that's for sure," said Reece, waving his coffee cup in front of Jesse's face. "Mind giving me another sip?"

"I think you've sipped yourself into a stupor. How about slowing down for a moment?"

"I'm in pain, Jesse. You said yourself it was the best thing for me."

Jesse rolled his eyes and prudently poured liquor into the cup. "Your gun shot is not going to be the only thing hurting in the morning. Go on Griff."

"By the time we could get up those cliffs, the last man was gone. Not a trace of him to be found."

"So, there is one still out there?" Grace asked.

"He won't last long," Reece said. "I think he was hurt. Coyotes can smell blood from miles away. A pack of them can tear a man apart. I plan to go back up there and see if I can find what's left of him as soon as I'm feeling better."

"Are these the same outlaws the Denver sheriff was talking about?" Jesse asked, taking Reece's cup away and adjusting the pillow behind his head. "We heard from your sheriff friend up there. He gave us a little background on these Bannisters that's going to be of interest to you."

"Lance and I recognized them from a poster," said Griff. "Looks like the old man, and his son, Luke, were killed. The other son, Lamont, is still on the loose."

"How do you think my father is involved?" Grace asked with a look of dread on her face. She hated to think that her family might be involved in cattle rustling or anything else illegal. It would be devastating to know Griff and other ranchers like him were hurt by her relatives.

"Grace had another dream last night," Griff said, speaking to Reece. "She believes she knew Lamont Bannister when they were young. She also thinks he and his family killed her father.

"I have no idea how this affects you, Grace," Reece said. "That may take some time to learn the rest of their story. Give me a little longer and I promise to find the truth." His head was spinning and it was obvious he was growing weaker by the minute. "Right now, I need some sleep." He closed his eyes for a moment before Griff and Jesse helped him into the bedroom.

Grace looked at the wanted poster still sitting on the table. The eyes of Luther Bannister were staring back at her. She could hear his raspy voice ringing through her ears and brushed her neck remembering his hot breath as he called her girlie. He was gone and would not bother her again. Perhaps now the dreams would cease.

CHAPTER 11

DENVER NEWS

"Saturday night," Tom Kelly bellowed.

"Pa, you know Doctor Larson left strict orders for you to stay off that leg or it will never heal."

Rachel set a serving tray on the table next to the chair where her father sat. Her cantankerous patient was growing more irritable with each passing day. He was a proud man and found it difficult to admit that the healing process, after the removal of a bullet deeply embedded in his thigh, required more ambulatory care than he had expected. Tom insisted he was perfectly capable of resuming his duties around the ranch.

"I've got work to do, little girl," he grumbled. "I can't spend my days laying around in bed. Besides, I think a celebration is in order."

He tried to hide the pain he felt in his leg when Lance grabbed him around the chest and hoisted him to a standing position so Rachel could fluff the pillows used to support his back. She did the same with the ones placed on the ottoman, then motioned for Lance to help their father sit again.

"Pa, that's a lot of work," said Rachel looking frazzled as she scurried to the window and opened the shade then hurried back to refill the water glass before placing the tray on her father's lap. "We're all doing the best we can and to take on the extra planning for a party is a bit much right now."

"Nonsense, it won't be that difficult. Margaret will help. She's been chomping at the bit to be in charge of something. Her and that garden club, sending food and flowers. I'd plan it myself if you didn't have me strapped to this chair. Matt and Griffin will put that beef on the pit. Better yet, set Jesse to doing that task. Your freshly baked bread, a couple of those fancy dishes Margaret always concocts. Lance says Grace's blackberry cobbler is tasty. We've got a whole garden full of vegetables to choose from. Mary Bernard's pies. You'll have plenty of help. Get Elizabeth involved. It will give me a chance to spend some time with my little granddaughter."

"I admit, it would be fun but we're already stretched. You know I love parties but Lance is pulling double duty at the ranch. Even with Matt and Griff trying to do their share to help it's up to the two of us to keep things going. A barbecue would take some doing. Besides, Doctor Larson says you need your rest."

"I'd be out of this chair right now if you'd stop fretting over me. I'm learning to use those crutches to get around. Reece is on the mend and I don't hear anyone talking about how Deputy Vance needs to stay in bed and rest."

"John Vance is my age Pa and built like a brick house. Of course, no one is worried about him resting," said Lance as he handed his father the newspaper. "Rachel's got a point."

"We should all congratulate ourselves. We have successfully tracked down two of the three men who rustled our cattle and when the third one is captured, or found dead as Reece predicts, then

Grace's terror will finally be over. A barbecue is just the thing we need. Besides, I'm not talking about anything big. Just a few of our friends."

"Pa, you just listed thirty people. How is that small? We might as well invite the entire county. I'm not sure Grace is ready for another outing after the last one. You're forgetting that she's had her hands full helping Griff take care of Reece."

"I'll have enough beef to feed the entire county now that I'm no longer losing cattle and I should think that young lady would enjoy getting out around people again. It'll do her good. We're hosting a barbeque on Saturday night for our friends and that's final."

Rachel looked at Lance who shrugged his shoulders. "You're exasperating, Pa, but if that's what you want. You have to promise to stay off that leg until Saturday night or I'll have Doctor Larson give you something to knock you out for the next month." She kissed her father on his head. "Do we have to invite the Richters? After what Clara put Grace through at the social, I don't think they deserve an invitation."

"Of course, we're inviting Henry and his family. He's a friend and I wouldn't dare insult him by leaving him off the guest list. I don't care what kind of arguments you girls have had. The Richters are going to be invited."

"I have to agree with Rachel on this one," said Lance. Not one to argue with his father, Lance seldom spoke up. He usually left it up to his older siblings to conflict with their father's wishes. He knew the trouble Clara caused Griff and felt she was partially to blame for what happened to Grace at the social.

Although most of the family agreed it was best the Bannisters showed up when they did, instead of waylaying his brother and Grace on the way home, he still held a resentment for Clara. He didn't like the way she and her friends treated Grace. He wasn't anxious to have her attend the barbecue either.

"This is more than just some girlish rivalry, Pa. She's been making a nuisance of herself where Griff is concerned for a long time. Any other man would have put her in her place by now, but you know Griff isn't the kind to do that. He respects your friendship with Mr. Richter and has always tried to be cordial to Clara but that woman is trouble and said some pretty horrible things about Grace."

"I know that Clara is a handful," admitted Tom. "Too uppity if you ask me. Never really cared for her myself and never understood why Griffin got involved with her in the first place but, that was his business. It's over with now and I'm sure Henry understands that, even if his daughter doesn't. If your sister can't bring herself to act like a well-mannered hostess and welcome everyone then she'll just have to spend the evening pouting in her room. For the last time, Henry Richter is invited to the barbecue and I won't have any more discussion. Come sit beside your pa, Rachel and we'll talk more about these plans."

Lance glanced at his sister and shrugged his shoulders again then recited the list of chores still left undone and with a sense of urgency excused himself to finish his day's work, scurrying out of the room before being drawn back into the conversation about the evils of Clara Richter. Rachel gave him a sour look in return before clattering around the house looking for paper and pencil. She plopped down beside her father exhaling loudly, poised to begin anew the argument over the size of the guest list. She knew her father was right but was just as stubborn as him. She also knew that Margaret Spencer was just the person to turn to if there was a party to be planned.

⅄

Griff dropped the saddle on the floor, waving at the air while muffling a choking cough as a puff of dust emanated from the leather when it hit the wooden planks. He threw his hat on the table and wiped his brow, frowning at the sofa where Reece, stretched out from end to end, casually reclined, watching Grace sew a replacement button on his shirt.

"Need some help there, buddy? I'd hate to see you wear out your backside from spending too much time relaxing on my sofa."

Reece stretched his arms and smugly smiled. Knowing it irked his friend to see him spend so much time with Grace, he grinned as if he was on the verge of snatching the prize trophy at the county fair. She was a diligent nurse. Washing his chest and changing his bandages, mortified that the wound in his side might develop infection. He was growing use to breakfast in bed and her pleasant company as she sat beside him, reading. Reece enjoyed the attention of his caretaker while watching Griff stomp around the house banging doors, mumbling under his breath.

He knew Griff didn't begrudge him the time he stayed there. Reece had no family to care for him and despite their bickering like an old married couple, they shared the bonds of a strong friendship forged out of lonely childhood experiences. The friends loved to aggravate each other but would never intentionally do harm.

"I've been thinking that I might be well enough to head on home but I know Grace would miss this opportunity to pamper me. I'm hanging around for her sake."

Grace raised her head with a look of denial then smiled before lowering her eyes again and nimbly pulling the needle through the fabric.

"Isn't that nice of my friend to be so accommodating? What would we do without him?"

"Griffin," Grace scolded, without glancing up. "Why have you thrown that dirty saddle on my clean floor.

"That dirty saddle belongs to you."

She set the shirt to the side and stood, hesitantly walking toward the saddle, lying by the door. Kneeling beside it, she ran her fingers over the smooth surface of the leather.

"It's been sitting in the barn since Lance brought it back from town the day of the stand-off at the cliffs. With all that's gone on, I was waiting for a good time to show you."

He touched Grace on the shoulder to break the trance she was lost in. Holding out one hand he helped her up, grabbing the saddle with the other. "I wanted Reece to have a clear mind, also."

Griff crossed the floor and set the saddle on the table, ushering Grace to her chair again. "Not that our sheriff ever has a clear mind, if he indeed, has a mind at all."

"That's jealousy talking," grinned Reece as he sprang to a sitting position and pulled the saddle closer. "I forgot all about this."

"I also picked up the mail for you when I was in town this morning," Griff handed an envelope to Reece. "You'll be happy to know that nothing's been set ablaze since you've been gone. Pa is having a barbecue, Saturday night. This news, according to Margaret. She ran me down on my way out of the post office."

"A barbecue?" said Grace, beaming. "That sounds exciting. I wonder if Rachel will let me borrow another dress. I didn't do a very good job of taking care of the last one."

"She'll never miss it. Margaret said Rach is planning to stop by and tell you about all the plans so act surprised when she gets here."

"More information from the Denver sheriff," Reece said, reading the letter. "The saddle was purchased from someone named Allister Neal, living there in Denver. He claims a man named John Cooper sold it to him. Mr. Neal says it was a good quality saddle which is why he bought it, but now he's decided he didn't care for it after all."

"Could this be my John?" asked Grace.

"If it is, how did he come to get your saddle?" Griff said. "John Cooper writes you a goodbye letter and leaves town. You show up half dead, shot down by the Bannisters and John Cooper winds up with the saddle from your horse, which was found grazing in a pasture with a saddlebag full of your belongings tossed in the weeds nearby. No one else around. The miner sells the saddle along with the horse to separate men in Carson City. Deputy Vance buys the horse from the gentleman who resides there and the saddle, purchased, we have to assume, by Cooper, shows up 600 hundred miles away in Colorado." He looked at Reece with a skeptical eye and knew the sheriff shared his thoughts. "That's a heck of a trip for a saddle. Strikes me as a little odd."

"More than a little odd. Not much of it makes sense," said Reece rubbing his forehead, deep in thought. "I'd say someone isn't telling the whole truth."

"But if Mr. Neal bought the saddle from John Cooper he would know where to find him. All we need to do is find John Cooper. That's been my goal the whole time. Who cares how he got the saddle. This is very good news. Griff, can we go to Denver?"

"The sheriff says Allister Neal doesn't know the whereabouts of John Cooper," said Reece, glancing at the letter again. "Neal claims he never saw him again after he bought the saddle. No one else in town knows anything about him either. It's like he's disappeared. Neal is under the impression Cooper might be an investor of some sort. I think it's a little premature to go running up to Denver."

"Maybe it's not my saddle after all."

"It's yours alright. Take a look at the cantle." Griff pointed to the raised back of the seat. "It has the same rose design as your saddle bag. That's not a coincidence. It has seen a lot of miles lately for not being strapped to the back of horse."

Reece examined the saddle, rubbing his hands over the roses burned into the leather then turned it upside down. "It's well made. Looks broken in so you must enjoy riding, Grace. We'll have to try it out soon." He winked and smiled making Grace blush before catching Griff's annoyed scowl. "All three of us, of course."

"This saddle has been a big part of your dreams. This and that filly of yours," said Griff, turning the saddle upright again. "There's a story behind this flower design. I'm kind of surprised your name isn't Rose. Did you ever hear that name?"

"No, I wondered about it when you first brought the saddlebag to me, but nothing is familiar. Maybe it was a favorite flower."

"It'll come to you in time," said Reece. "As for now, I believe I'm the one who's going to have to take that trip to Denver and call on Allister Neal. I've got a few questions and I can't get a good feel for any of this until I look him straight in the eye." He stood and stretched again, yawning as he looked around. "If you're about through sewing that button on, I think I'll pack up my things."

"You're not leaving, are you?" Grace stood and held out the shirt. "We haven't had lunch and we have all this news about John Cooper. What if the Bannisters found him, like they found me?"

"I've neglected my work long enough. I think I'm well enough to get started on some of these clues we've got. I've put off finding Lamont Bannister too because I believe he's dead. It's time I head up into the hills to make sure."

"You think I'm finally safe now?" asked Grace. "If you think he's dead then why bother?"

"I think you're as safe as you've ever been while under our care," Reece grinned. "I have a mind not to look but I believe that Bannister deserves a decent burial no matter what he's done. I might even try to find that spot where the miner found your horse. Maybe there was something else tossed in the brush besides your saddle bag. I don't know why I haven't done it before now. You and Griff have done enough for me and if I leave Vance in charge much longer, the town will run wild."

"You'll be back in time for the barbeque, won't you? Everyone is expecting you. I'm sure Mr. Kelly would be disappointed." Grace looked at Griff with pleading eyes as if he could persuade the sheriff to change his mind.

"He's not going to miss the barbecue, Grace," said Griff grinning. "Reece Cameron has never turned down a good meal in his life. Especially when it's prime beef from the Emerald ranch. You can count on him to be first in line at the food table.

"I promise to be back in time, if you promise me another dance."

"You're a brave man, Reece Cameron," Grace laughed. "I'd be surprised if your feet aren't still sore from the last time. I don't think I'll ever be very good."

"You did fine. You're just out of practice." Reece grabbed Grace around the waist and pulled her into his arms. Humming a favorite tune, he lifted her off her feet and swung her around.

"Reece," Grace squealed as he twirled her across the room. Her dress flew up as they danced, her white petticoat fluttering, showing much more than a lady should. She laughed unabashedly at her appearance while happily spinning through the air.

"Grace," Griff shouted.

Reece stopped turning and set her down. She grabbed her side, aching from laughter, suddenly aware of Griff's stern glare. "I guess we got carried away," she said, trying not to laugh.

"She's self-conscious. I wanted to make her feel more confident. I think that did the trick."

"Serves you right if you bust those stitches in your side from swinging her around like that," said Griff.

"That's just more jealous talk," replied Reece, still grinning. "Don't let him fool you, Grace. He would have done the same thing if he thought of it first."

"I have more sense than to take that chance. Do you need someone to keep you company tomorrow when you go up into those hills? I'm not kidding about those stitches. If you run into trouble, you'll be weak."

"Both of you?" Grace asked, disappointed that Griff would volunteer to go along with Reece. "There won't be anyone left to go to the barbecue. I guess I should tell Jesse to shine up the surrey again."

Na, I appreciate the offer but I'll be fine. I can still shoot and ride although maybe a little slower. You better stay here and practice your dancing with Grace. I'll be expecting to see her twirl across that floor like a ballerina when I get back. Besides, sounds like Tom is going to need your help for Saturday."

"Don't worry about Grace's twirling and save that trip to find where her filly was left. We'll go next week. Try not to come back with another bullet in your side."

Grace spent the rest of the day in her room. She wanted some time alone to think about her future. The Bannisters were gone and like it or not, they were a link to her past. With their death, the chance to know her identity might be lost. Her wounds were healed and she couldn't continue to stay at the Emerald as an unmarried woman. Despite Griff's annoyance with Reece's antics, when it came to the battle for her attentions, he had never spoken about a future together. If he was not interested in a serious relationship with her then Grace felt there was no other choice but to create a life on her own.

Griff had once suggested she could stay with his family at the Kelly ranch if she felt more comfortable and perhaps that was a good option. Maybe the Spencers would agree to take her in as a border until she could find a way to support herself. Either situation would be a more respectable arrangement and would give her time to sort out where what she wanted to do with the rest of her life.

She would not stop until she found John Cooper. If he was indeed the man who had once been her fiancé, then he would be able to tell her about the past and it would all finally be laid to rest. She needed to be the one to visit with Alistair Neal in Denver and not Reece. No one could stop her from riding out on her own but a woman traveling alone on horseback might not be safe. If she sold her horse and saddle, she could take the stage and have enough money to travel to Colorado, find Mr. Neal, track down John Cooper and end this mystery.

She picked up the picture of her mother, resting in the small oval frame on the night stand and wondered what the woman was like. Did she come west with her husband as Eleanor Kelly had? Grace knew in her heart why no one had come looking for her. There was no one left to care. After the barbecue, she would send a message to Allister Neal in Denver and inform him of her impending arrival. Then, no longer the girl named Grace, she would become Anne once more.

CHAPTER 12

FIGHTING LIFE'S BATTLES

Tom Kelly sat on the ladder back arm chair, a single crutch leaning against the side of the house. Will Spencer rested comfortably beside him in the cane seat of a matching chair, legs crossed, head nodding in agreement as Tom explained what effect an early winter would have on the health of his cattle.

The veranda was already bustling with garden club members streaming in and out of the house like a trail of ants. They followed each other, in a straight line down the steps, veering off onto a brick pathway leading through an arbor toward a large juniper tree where long wooden tables stood closely pulled together in a horseshoe design.

Once there, they would look to Margaret for instruction as she directed the group like a maestro at an orchestra symposium. The edges of white cotton tablecloths waved gently in the late summer breeze, occasionally flipping, haphazardly, up and onto the table. Margaret would mutter and call for a heavy bowl to be placed near a corner to hold down the flapping covering.

Matt and Lance set up chairs in groups of three or four, circling the tree. They would stop briefly to eye the sun, guessing if the outstretched branches of the old juniper would still offer a cool respite as the afternoon grew longer. If there was any doubt, they would scoot the seats to the right or left before surveying the sky again.

Griff turned the handle of the spit suspended over reddened embers watching the beef slowly brown, pausing long enough for Jesse to dip his brush into a bowl of sauce and paint the meat with spicy liquid

"Margaret keeping you busy?" asked Tom as Grace appeared on the porch accompanied by Rachel and Elizabeth Kelly. The pretty blonde woman, married to Griff's brother, Matt, adjusted the weight of the little girl perched on her right hip before finally setting the child down.

"We're about as ready as we can be, Pa. Elizabeth and I were going to walk through Mama's garden. Margaret has charged us with recruiting Grace for membership in the club."

"We're hoping she's a better horticulturist than us, " added Elizabeth. "We've already explained the work involved in maintaining Eleanor's floral retreat she started years ago."

"I'm glad you girls are taking the time to get to know each other. Elizabeth has meant so much to us since she and Matt were married. She's wanted him to take her to visit you but, of course, none of us wanted to impose when you were sick. I'm counting on Griffin to bring you back on a regular basis now that you're feeling well again."

"It's an honor to be invited, Mr. Kelly."

"You've met our little Hope, of course," said Tom, reaching out for the toddler and cuddling her on his lap. "She loves her old Papa, don't you?"

"The little girl leaned her head on Tom's shoulder and snuggled in his arms.

"My Eleanor had quite a talent when it came to growing flowers. Of course, Eleanor had a talent for just about anything she put her mind to. I guess Rachel told you that my wife and Margaret Spencer started the garden club years ago when we first moved to this house. She planted that garden a bit at a time. Use to call it her little retreat. She always said it cleared her mind when she spent time there. Matt helped me build that arbor and she planted those morning glories around it. I think it's the prettiest sight when they are in bloom, growing up through that lattice work. I wanted to cut that old juniper down but she wouldn't let me. "

"I'm anxious to see it, Mr. Kelly. I'm sure Rachel and Elizabeth have done a wonderful job in keeping it perfect."

"You girls take Grace on down and show her what you've done. Will and I will watch Hope. I'd go with you too but no one in this family thinks I need to be walking too much on this leg."

"Don't let her wear you out, Tom. I'll send Matt to get her when he and Lance are finished with the chairs," said Elizabeth. "We won't be gone long. People are starting to arrive now. We need to be here to greet them."

"That's what Will and I are for. You take your time."

Grace waved at Griff as the women strolled by, passing through the arbor on their way to the garden. He smiled and waved back before jumping to safety when Jesse's abundant scoop of sauce dripped from the simmering beef onto the coals, sending a spiral of flames in the air.

"This was my mother's favorite spot," said Rachel, stopping by a bench bordered by rose bushes. Grace bent over to smell the blooms and her attention was drawn to letters scratched deep in the wooden seat.

"I see you've noticed the initials," said Rachel, embarrassed at the jagged edges of letters carved in each corner. "You can thank Griff for this, I guess. He was twelve when Pa built that bench for mama. She loved roses and planted these bushes. She pointed to a large G and k obviously scrawled by a child. "Griff decided to carve his initials into the seat. When Pa saw what he had done, he went through the roof."

"But there are four sets of initials."

"Not originally. It was just Griff's in the beginning. He claims it was Matt's idea. According to him, Matt egged him on and told Griff my mother would just love it."

"Was your mother mad?" chuckled Grace.

"She was disappointed at first but mama wasn't one to stay mad at any of us too long. She said it added character to the bench and made it even more special. So, turns out, we all got to carve our initials, eventually. "

Rachel pointed to the M and K. "Matt put his there in the right corner and mine are on the bottom left. Lance got the only spot left. My mother always wanted Pa to put a big heart in the middle of the seat but then she got sick and…well...he never got around to it after that."

"It is unique that's for sure," said Grace. "Something a mother would love. Do you think Hope will get to do the same someday? Looks like there is still room. It could start a family tradition."

"Tom would let her do anything, " laughed Elizabeth. " Let's not give her any ideas."

"Don't fill her head with all these stories, you two. Leave me with some respect." Griff appeared behind the women, smiling. He picked a blossom from one of the rose bushes and handed it to Grace. "None of it is true and if it is, then you can blame Matt. He was always goading me into doing something stupid but I swear, I was purely innocent."

"Oh, Griff," said Elizabeth, shaking her head. "I wasn't around when you two were growing up, but I can guarantee if there was trouble brewing, you were just as guilty as your brother."

"Now Elizabeth, you've been brainwashed. Every time we got into trouble, Matt walked away unscathed and I got to take the trip to the wood shed."

"Pa even took a switch to Reece a couple of times, I think," said Rachel. "Once, he accidently set fire to a bale of hay Pa set out for the horses. Using a magnifying glass. Pa was afraid the whole pasture would go up in flames."

"I thought we were all going to get it that time," laughed Griff. "I think the worst was when Reece and I set off that string of firecrackers outside the church window during Sunday service. We added an extra-long fuse so we would have time to get inside and sit down before they went off."

"The entire congregation jumped off their seats at the same time," said Rachel. "Lance was small and started screaming."

"Old Miss Hamilton ran down the center aisle waving her hands in the air like a lunatic, yelling the Yankees were coming and we were all going to be killed," Griff snickered.

Rachel hit her brother on the arm and tried her best to frown before exploding into laughter. "That was horrible. The poor woman lived through the siege of Atlanta when the union army burned it to the ground and every time she heard loud gunfire she fell to pieces."

"Once again, it was Matt's idea. He sat in church laughing at it all but in the end, it was me and Reece that were headed for another trip to the wood shed. I don't even think Pa waited until we got home. He took us out back of the church and swatted us both there. Pa always said that Reece spent so much time at our house he was just like one of his own and would get a walloping just like the rest of us."

"No one escapes the wrath of my father, when he gets mad," said Rachel

"Funny that Reece turned out to be a sheriff after all the things he did when you two were young," said Elizabeth. "I'm surprised both of you didn't end up on the other side of those jail bars. And I've heard the fireworks story, before. I believe Matt got his punishment from your father, later. They were his fireworks, after all."

"I told you, no one escapes," laughed Rachel.

"I came to escort you beautiful young ladies back to the house. People are milling around ready to eat and Margaret doesn't want to let them start without Rachel's blessing. You know most of the guests from the church social, Grace. Mrs. Ferguson and Juanita and Jeb Miller. Most of the garden club women. Rach and Elizabeth will introduce you to the rest. I'm going to make sure Jesse doesn't need help with the rest of the meat."

Griff led the women back to the large framed country home. The wrap-around porch was filled with people hovering around Tom as he sat with Hope in his lap. Matt waved to get their attention and motioned them toward the tables of food where a line was starting to form.

"I'll join you in a couple of minutes," said Griff, squeezing Grace's hand before walking off toward the fire pit. "Keep her away from Clara," he whispered to Rachel. "We don't need a repeat of the social."

"I believe Tom has outdone himself this time. I don't see an unhappy face in the crowd." Will Spencer appeared and stood next to the fire, watching Griff stir the dying embers. "I've been sent to retrieve you."

"I was just about to go back. I wanted to make sure this fire didn't start up again. We have Margaret to thank for helping with the success of the barbecue."

Holding a plate with one hand, Will sliced through the corner of a piece of apple pie and shoveled it onto the edge of the fork. "She's not the only one that did the work. Rachel was really the one who organized this bash. It's a tribute to her, the way she has grown into such a fine young lady. Tom is lucky to have her. Of course, he knows it."

He cut another corner off the pie and placed it in his mouth. "Your young lady seems to blend right in. Margaret's infatuated with her. The rest of the garden club seem so too. She's a pretty girl."

"Well, count me in with the infatuated group," answered Griff. "She seems to be comfortable here, doesn't she?"

"Tom says you're pretty fond of this young lady. I think he's expecting you to make some sort of formal announcement, soon. You know Margaret is going to want to throw a party when that happens. It gives her comfort to see all of you settle down with families of your own. She and your mother use to talk about the day when there would be weddings to plan."

Griff smiled and glanced toward the veranda where Grace stood talking with Elizabeth and his brother. "Well Margaret might be getting a little ahead of herself. I am very fond of Grace and I've been giving some thought to...well you know... just thinking about the future. I'm not sure the time is right. She's been through so much it seems like every day is a new crisis for us to deal with. I'm not sure Grace would be ready."

"Griffin, Margaret and I have been married thirty years come September. There have been very few weeks in our life when we haven't faced some sort of crisis. That's what marriage is all about. Finding that one person you want to fight those battles with. Trusting each other to stick with you no matter how good or how bad it gets. That's what Tom and Eleanor did. It's what we all do. Margaret and I have had our share of sorrow. We lost our boy, William."

Will paused and stared at the fire, clearing his throat before beginning again. "But we've had many days of happiness. Life can get lonely without someone to share it with but it can be wonderful if you find that special person. If you have the right kind of feelings for that young woman then my advice is to snatch her up before someone else does. Now that the Bannisters are taken care of, you have nothing standing in your way."

"That reminds me, Will. I meant to ask you something. Have you ever heard of a man named John Cooper? He's some kind of investor. Might have worked in Nevada and possibly set up a business in Denver recently?"

"John Cooper," repeated Will. He stabbed at the last bite of pie and stuffed it in his mouth, chewing quietly. "An investor, you say?"

"That's what Reece and I were led to believe. We think he might be connected to Grace somehow, could have been her fiancé."

"The gentleman who wrote her the letter?"

"That's the one."

"Griffin, you're sure this man was an investor?"

"Reece got a letter from the Denver sheriff who stated he found someone who had met John Cooper."

"I have heard of the man and I'm afraid it's not good news. It would certainly be reason for concern if Grace were involved with him. Does she recall the name?"

"Not a thing. What do you know about him?"

Margaret and I were in San Francisco about a year ago. We had dinner one night with some people from the cattleman's association. They talked of a man named John Cooper who was involved in moving stolen cattle."

"Is he a rustler? I wonder if Grace's family was mixed up with him and possibly the Bannisters. She'll be devastated if that was the case."

"No, his kind never get their hands dirty," Will replied. "He's the broker, the brains of the operation. Forcing small ranchers to sell out, then using their land to hold the stolen cattle. They dealt in horses too from what I heard. This Cooper fellow is wanted from Abilene to Sacramento."

"I can't believe it, Will. How can she be mixed up with someone like him? Did she know what kind of man he was?"

"If they were engaged as you say. Are you sure of this, Griffin?"

"According to the letter we found in her saddle bag they are or at least they were. The point of the letter was him breaking off the engagement and that he was grateful to her father. He said he was on his way to Denver but according to the sheriff there, no one has seen or heard from him. To think that Grace might be mixed up with murderers and thieves."

"I wouldn't jump to conclusions, Griff. From what I understand, John Cooper is a dangerous man and wherever he is, I think it would be better for Grace if he stayed gone. Your Grace was lucky to get away with her life. Whatever it is, the Bannisters were looking for, I wouldn't be surprised if Cooper wasn't behind it which means she may not be out of danger yet. Why don't you let me contact my San Francisco people and make a few inquiries? Don't let this spoil your evening."

Griff swallowed hard and gave Will a faint smile. "I've been cooking this meat all day and I haven't gotten to eat a bite. I think I better fill a plate with some of that good food the ladies have set out before it's all been eaten by the likes of you."

"Well then, I better get another piece of pie before you start in," Will laughed.

Laughter erupted as Grace walked in the front door of the Kelly house. Glancing in the parlor, she found John Vance recovering from the injury incurred during the gunfire with the Bannisters that day at the cliffs. He sat comfortably in the overstuffed chair, usually reserved for Tom, with his bandaged leg propped up on a footstool surrounded by a bevy of young ladies.

Lance stood before the group, entertaining them with stories of heroism during the shootout. His exaggerated animation in describing the adventures of young deputy Vance enthralled the female listeners and delighted his friend.

"There he was," Lance whispered to the young women as they sat entranced, breathlessly waiting for his next word. "Riddled with bullets, and nearly blind from the pain, our hero scaled the dangerous wall of the cliffs."

Five pairs of wide eyes stared at Lance, his hands reaching up, clawing at the air as he reenacted Vance's climb. "Suddenly he sees the dastardly criminals and stops."

One of the young ladies clutched her friend's arm and gasped as Lance continued in a hushed voice. "Our beloved Deputy raised his gun and aimed, but just as he did, a rock gave way and he lost his grip, leaving him dangling by one hand."

The women squealed and clung to each other unable to move. John Vance rolled his eyes and fought to maintain his stoic face as he comforted the young ladies by patting as many pretty shoulders as he could reach from his relaxed position on the chair.

Grace shook her head and chuckled as she walked on, knowing that in truth, John Vance was shot at the beginning of the gun battle and, because of his injuries, never made it to the cliff with the others. Scanning the room, she couldn't find Rachel among the guests who had wandered in after eating but spotted Elizabeth in the corner, sitting at the piano and decided to join her.

"Do you mind if I sit with you for a moment? I was looking for Rachel but must have missed her."

"Please do. We haven't had a chance to talk much." Elizabeth scooted to the side and Grace slid in beside her. "Do you play?"

"No, but I'd love to learn. Of course, if it's anything like my dancing skills I'm afraid a teacher would give up on me quickly."

"I never learned until I moved here. I grew up on a farm and there never seemed to be much time for things like music. When I came to Nevada I met a man…a friend I should say, who played beautifully. Worked on a river boat after the war. He promised to teach me but had to leave town rather suddenly so never got the chance. Matt talked the church organist into giving me lessons. I must say I'm not perfect but it's very relaxing for me." Elizabeth struck an awkward chord and laughed. "Except when I hit a wrong note."

"It sounded wonderful to me. The organist must be a good teacher."

"Mary Bernard," said Elizabeth, shuffling through sheet music piled on top of the piano.

"Mary Bernard the famous pie baker?"

"The very same. That woman can do anything. She and Margaret Spencer. I don't know that it's fair for those two to have soaked up all the talent in the world while the rest of us just stumble carelessly along. I'd be glad to show you what I know. Unless you want Mary to teach you. She'd love to do it, I'm sure."

"I don't know where I'd practice and Griff has done so much already, I wouldn't dare ask him to buy a piano just for me."

"I don't think he'd give it a second thought. From what I can see, all you have to do is ask."

Grace blushed and looked away. Elizabeth, like the rest of the Kellys, was a woman who spoke her mind. She'd heard stories from Griff about the courtship of his brother and this petite woman with the blue eyes that mesmerized Matt from the moment they met. Elizabeth had a different air about her than Rachel. More serious and independent. She thought they might be good friends had they known each other in the past.

"I'm sorry I missed you at the church social, I'm sure by now you've heard of the mess it turned out to be," Grace picked up a piece of music and stared at the scales of notes.

"Rachel filled me in," Elizabeth smiled. "Don't be embarrassed. Clara Richter and her catty friends are responsible for hurting the feelings of many. Me included. She suggested I was a poor country girl after the Kelly money."

"That's awful," Grace said. "According to her, I'm a loose woman living in sin. Her friends said no man would marry someone like me."

"Don't pay any attention to those two gossipy hens. They couldn't catch a husband if they tied a man to a church pew and held a gun to the preacher's head. They're jealous and so is Snooty Hooty, Clara. She's had her eye on Griffin for years and she can't stand it because he is in love with you."

"Snooty Hooty," Grace giggled. "That's what Rachel calls her. She quickly looked around the room to see who might be close enough to overhear their conversation. "Do you think that Griff?"

"You can't tell me you're surprised? It's written all over his face. Lance and Rachel have mentioned it. Even Tom noticed and he never notices anything. I'm surprised Margaret hasn't dragged you into town to order a wedding dress. The minute I saw you two together, I told Matt that his brother had finally found the right girl."

"I admit it's something I've thought of but he's never spoken a word about what might happen once my memory comes back. I've been afraid to get my hopes up about the future. How could I be so stupid?"

Grace thought of her plans for Denver. According to Elizabeth, Griff loved her but she still needed an explanation for all that had happened. She would not be deterred from trying to find John Cooper. So, she would seek out Allister Neal in Denver and make one last attempt to solve the puzzle and if she could not, she would return, content to know that the events which unfolded since she and Griff met had led her to happiness.

"Elizabeth, if you will excuse me, I need to find Griffin. He's probably wondering what's taking me so long." Grace gave her a hug before jumping up from the bench. "I've enjoyed our talk more than you can know. Should you and I not have a chance to see each other again for a while, please know I'm thankful for the friendship you've shown me."

Elizabeth stood, looking confused as Grace started to walk away. "I'm sure we'll see each other soon. Don't forget about the piano lessons."

Grace walked down the steps to find Griff waiting. "I haven't had a chance to dance with my girl all night," he said. "Let's get to it before those fiddlers get tired and go home." He grabbed her hand and pulled her through the crowd to the dance floor. "Are you enjoying yourself?'

"Yes. This is a wonderful home. You must have had some childhood growing up here."

"My parents tried to make it nice for us. There was some hard work to go along with it. Long days when we were on a trail drive with Pa."

Griff swung Grace around as they danced and spotted Clara Richter out of the corner of his eye, standing by the punch table, scanning the crowd. He was determined to keep his distance from her and the punch table for the rest of the evening and quickly steered

Grace in the opposite direction, running her into the back of Sheriff Cameron and Rachel.

"Reece, you made it," Grace said, excitedly. "You kept your word."

"I told you he wouldn't miss a meal. I see you brought your own dance partner too."

"I found the little Kelly sister standing by herself and felt obliged to dance a time or two," Reece laughed.

"Ugh," grunted Rachel. "Must you always call me that?"

"I've called you that since you were five. I don't see a need to change now. I'm wondering if there is a reason why your brother felt he needed to run over us while we're out here socializing?"

"There is, but I'll explain later," said Griff, trying to nonchalantly motion toward the punch table. "How was your trip? Looks like you made it back in one piece."

"Well, it was the thought of all this food. I couldn't let you eat it all.?"

"Will Spencer and I had an interesting conversation earlier, if you could tear yourself away from your socializing for a few minutes, I'd like to go over a few things."

"What is it Griff?" Is it something I should know?" asked Grace.

"Will was telling me about a trip he and Margaret took to San Francisco last year. I thought Reece might enjoy hearing about it. Would you and Rachel mind sitting out the next dance? We won't be long."

"I was looking for you, Grace," said Rachel. "I was hoping to introduce you to a friend of mine. She couldn't make it to the church social and she's heard so much about you, she'll be disappointed if you get away again without having a chance to say hello. Griff can catch up in a few minutes."

Grace smiled inquisitively before turning and walking toward the house with Rachel. She suspected Griff had information for Reece concerning her or was hoping Reece had uncovered something and they were hesitant to tell her. She wanted to stay and pressure them into including her in the conversation but the barbecue wasn't the place to force this issue so instead, she decided to trust that Griff knew what he was doing. He had always been honest with her about everything involving the Bannisters and there was no reason to doubt him now.

Griff led Reece to the barn where they found Lance sitting on a bale of hay with John Vance enjoying a bottle of whiskey. The two had run out of daring stories for the ladies and retreated there away from the giggling women.

Vance was stretched out on the dirt floor, his leg propped up on a saddle when Griff walked in. He threw down another bale and settled in.

"Did you find Lamont Bannister rotting somewhere in the wild?" Griff finally asked.

"As a matter of fact, I did not," answered Reece. "It's surprising. Even if an animal got him, there should be something left. I guess there's a chance he might not be dead."

"You think he got smart and left the area?" asked Lance. "That's what I'd do. You wouldn't catch me within a hundred miles of this place."

"Maybe he knows someone in the area who was willing to hide him," said Vance. "He could be holed up someplace. Especially if he's wounded."

"It's a possibility. I'm not sure what to think of it."

"We may have bigger problems," Griff reached for the bottle Lance was holding and took a swig. "Will Spencer had heard the name John Cooper. He says the guy is about as crooked as they come. He's known for running a stolen cattle operation."

"Is he tied to the Bannisters?" asked Lance.

"It would make sense. Will says he's a dangerous man and wanted by the law in more than one state. He's going to contact an associate in San Francisco and see what else he can find out."

"You think this Cooper fellow might come looking for Grace? The Bannisters were hunting something they thought she had. Maybe this man is after the same thing." said Lance.

Reece took a deep breath and exhaled slowly. "It's something we have to consider at this point. It's got me worried"

"I wouldn't be surprised if the cattlemen have heard of the Bannisters too. They might be able to provide information about Grace," said Griff. "If her father was part of Cooper's organization, we could get a name, a town, something for her to go on."

"You think her father is involved?"

"I can't be sure but I don't want her to know any of this until we see what Will can find. I just can't see upsetting Grace before we have more of the story."

"I agree and I have an idea that I'm not sure you're going to like. It's something I thought about the whole way back today," Reece said. "I believe it's time to take Grace back up to the hills. If we walk her around the place where you found her, talk about the Bannisters, her horse and saddle, even that letter from Cooper. Maybe there is a chance it will jog her memory. Even if nothing is familiar at the time, she may dream about it later."

"After all that's happened, you want to put her through that?" Griff was amazed that his friend would suggest something like this. He knew Reece was right. It was time Grace went back to face that day again but Griff hated to watch her suffer.

"I'm willing if it helps get her memory back. You know she wants that more than anything. What do you think she would say if we asked her?" Reece said.

"I think she would want to go," Griff answered. "I can't believe she hasn't already thought of it. When do you want to take her?"

"Tomorrow. If she remembers something then maybe she can fill us in on John Cooper herself. I thought I'd stop by in the morning. She's been wanting to ride her horse. The three of us can go together. Make sure you bring the saddle bags and everything she found in it."

"You coming for breakfast? Grace is cooking."

"I'll be there bright and early."

"You walking back to the house with me?"

"No, I'm going to stay here with these two for a while." Reece reached for the whiskey Vance was holding.

"Yeah, we're great company," said Lance.

"That's debatable," said Griff as he started to leave. "Hey Reece. Do you think Grace still loves John Cooper? I mean, if she gets her memory back will she be broken hearted that he jilted her?"

"Not anymore, my friend," Reece smiled. He leaned back against the side of the hay bale and placed the bottle of whiskey to his lips. "Careful going home."

Grace sat in the parlor with Rachel and smiled when Griff returned. He knew it was getting late and Reece would be at the Emerald early. He reached for her hand, suggesting it might be time to leave. She gave Rachel a hug and said goodnight. Holding Griff's arm, they walked to the buggy and started home.

"Grace," Griff began when they had driven a distance from the Kelly ranch. "Reece is coming tomorrow for breakfast. He thought it would be nice if we saddled up your filly and the three of us go for a ride. It's something you've wanted to do."

She did not immediately answer. She was hoping they might go on a picnic. She wanted time alone to tell him how she felt. If Griff was afraid to speak about his feelings then she didn't mind being the first to say something.

"I thought the two of us might ride together. I was hoping we would have a chance to talk. A picnic would be nice."

"The truth is, Grace, we want to ride up to the hills. Reece has this crazy idea that it might help you remember. I told him I wouldn't force it so if you don't want to go we'll call the whole thing off."

"Oh, what made him think of that? Is there something I need to know?"

"Reece, feels like it's the obvious next step. We're stuck for what to do now."

"We could go to Denver and find Allister Neal."

"Reece is still planning to make that trip but first, we'd like to go up to the hills. It might be painful but you've faced everything thrown at you so far. I'll be there if it gets tough. I won't let it go too far. It's up to you."

"I guess that would be alright. If you two think it will help."

"I don't care if you ever get your memory back, Grace. It doesn't matter who you've known or what's happened in the past. I think you should understand that, but I also know that Reece has a point. I wouldn't suggest it if I didn't think it was a good idea."

"Then we'll go," Grace said, reaching for Griff's hand.

"We'll save the picnic for another day," Griff said. "We have plenty of time."

He squeezed her hand and smiled. This was the woman he let into his home and his heart. He wasn't going to give up on her now. No matter what lay ahead, it would be, as Will described, a battle they would fight together.

CHAPTER 13

BACK TO THE HILLS

Jesse led the black filly from the barn and tied her to the post by the front porch. She looked beautiful with her freshly brushed mane and sleek coat. The saddlebags hung loosely on each side, their rose design prominently displayed, adding graceful style to an already handsome animal.

Grace stood shivering in the cold and watched him check the straps on the saddle once again. She looked at her boot as she slid it in the stirrup. Blood stains were still visible on the worn leather and she hesitated for a moment before pulling herself up and onto the horse. She was dressed in pants and shirt reminiscent of those she'd worn the day she was found. It was Griff's effort to replicate as much as possible from that day. Now, after a quiet breakfast where little was spoken of the day's scheduled trip, Grace talked softly to her horse and waited for Reece and Griff to mount up.

"You three planning on being gone all day?" Jesse asked.

Grace shot a foreboding look at Griff and then Reece. After consenting to Reece's plan, she had slept little and knew from the sounds of pacing footsteps in the next room, that Griff had lost sleep as well.

"We'll be gone as long as it takes," replied Reece.

"Now see here, Reece," Jesse snapped, his eyes flaring. "This young woman has been through enough and I don't want you making this worse by dragging the whole thing out. If she remembers then fine but if..."

"Jesse, we've already had this discussion," Griff said, exasperated. "We know how you feel but none of us wants to hurt Grace. Going back could be the solution she's looking for. If it's too painful for her, then we're prepared to turn around and come back."

Jesse continued to glare at Reece, then walked over and patted Grace's leg. "Don't you let these two bully you into something you don't want to do."

"I won't," Grace said with a faint smile. "Don't worry Jesse, I'll be alright." She took a deep breath and turned to Griff. "Ready?"

No one spoke as the three turned their horses toward the road, each following in line past the barn and corral, through the gate and to the road that would take them into the hills. The morning fog hanging over the fields dissipated quickly, leaving the lush, green landscape of the Emerald ranch. Its gently rolling pastures scattered with grazing cattle eventually gave way to the rocky terrain Griff crossed weeks before. His thoughts were now focused on the morning he headed out alone in search of a cougar and he sensed the anxiety building in all of them as they grew closer to their destination.

"Let's stop and rest the horses. Watering holes are going to be scarce up ahead. I could use a cool drink myself," he said.

Grace climbed down without saying a word. She lifted the strap of her canteen from the saddle and carried it to the rocky edge of a pond. This small, isolated span of water, nursed few plants, leaving its shores uninviting to travelers. She took a drink and stared at the ground.

"Gets pretty quiet out here. Especially this early in the morning," said Griff, sitting beside her. I don't think the birds get up until noon."

Grace glanced up with a hint of a smile then pulled her knees to her chest and circled them with her arms, staring again at the rocky dirt below her. The stillness was broken when a hawk circled overhead, mournfully crying as it flew above, leaving Grace in a state of panic. She let out a shriek and jumped up, turning in all directions as if expecting to see Luther Bannister's menacing face behind her.

"Looks like I was wrong. That old hawk's out looking for his breakfast." Griff touched her hand and motioned for her to sit again. "He's not going to hurt anyone, unless it's a gopher he's spotted."

Grace smiled again and sat down, gazing at the water. You doing alright?" Griff asked "It won't be long until we're there. I'm right here with you, Grace."

Grace nodded and took another drink. "It's so lonely out here."

"It can be, but you're not alone. Remember that."

Once more they mounted and rode, single file toward the hills. Grace continually turned around in her saddle as they approached, expecting to see the ghostly shadows of advancing horses. The memory of their hoofs slamming on the rocky ground drowned out all other noises, leaving her anxious to get to their destination and safely away from the desolate open country they were crossing. It was an eerie feeling to be in this place where her life was nearly ended yet be unable to recognize a single stone or bush.

"This is where we need to stop," Griff said as he slowed his horse and began to dismount. He helped Grace down and hugged her, whispering that she was safe and not to be afraid. Guiding her toward a hill, they paused at the base. She surveyed the area, straining to find something familiar while Reece and Griffin watched her, not knowing what to expect.

"I found you here," Griff said, pointing to a huge bolder. "Based on this location, Reece and I figure you'd been running on foot for quite a while. You must have been worn down from the Bannisters chasing you. It was sunny that day, if I remember correctly and just past noon when I arrived. Judging by the way you looked at the time, I'd guess you'd been laying here a couple of hours."

"What a forsaken place this is," said Grace. "If you hadn't come along when you did, this rocky hill would have been the last thing I saw." She closed her eyes and tried to imagine the details of that day as Griff told his story.

"I thought it was an animal at first. I'd been expecting to find the remains of one of my calves. Rascal was jumpy. Even animals hate to come out here. I saw something at the bottom of the hill from back there." He pointed to brush in the distance from where they'd just traveled.

Grace was dizzy as she stood there with her eyes closed, listening to his narration. The images of three men flashed in her mind and the pounding in her head grew stronger. She was breathless as she imagined how it felt to run over the rough terrain on foot with the Bannisters in pursuit.

"You were barely breathing when I got to you. Your shirt was torn around that wound in your shoulder. Like the force of the bullet just blew the fabric apart. Your hair was full of blood."

"We think one of the Bannisters shot you here and you hit your head on the bolder when you fell," Reece added. "That's how you got that gash on your forehead."

Grace dropped to the ground, covering her ears with her hands. The image of three men riding fast grew vivid. Luther Bannister in the lead as they approached. She was perspiring and her breathing quickened as she relived that day. Whimpering, she remembered the run up the hill, falling, and the fear that she would soon be dead.

Griffin reached out for her hand but Reece pulled it back. Grace's memory was returning. Her expression of agony was proof that the door to secrets tightly held in her mind was opening and the visions, once only dreams, were awakened. He wanted no interruption by his friend, no matter how well intended.

"You got no place to hide, girlie," Reece cried out in a sinister voice.

Grace screamed as the memory of the Bannisters overwhelmed her. She could feel the searing pain as the bullet ripped through her flesh. Grabbing her shoulder, she rocked back and forth muttering, 'They're coming.'

Reece struggled to hold Griff back but he could no longer bear to watch Grace tormented and fought the sheriff to get free. Tearing away, he sat down, wrapping his arms around her until the shaking ceased.

"I was at the top of the hill when they shot me," Grace said, with her eyes still closed. "Lamont tried to stop them, but they wouldn't listen. I was laying here by this rock when Luther asked him if I was dead." She squinted as she looked up at Reece. Standing with his back toward the sun, it reminded her of the blurry figure of Lamont Bannister who had knelt beside her, closed her eyes and told her not to speak. "He saved my life."

"What else do you remember?" asked Reece.

Grace thought for a moment, searching her mind hoping for more visions to appear. "I remember a white house. It was on fire. Even now, I can smell the smoke and see scorching flames climbing to the roof. A man is pushing me out of the back door, shouting 'Run, they're coming'. I head toward the barn. My horse is waiting for me and I climb on." She paused for a moment taking a deep breath.

"You're safe, Grace," Griff whispers. "It's alright to remember. Nothing can harm you now." He brushed the hair from her face and smiled. "I'm with you, go on."

"I climb on the horse and dig my heels in her side. She gallops away, as if she knows the danger." Grace leans on Griff's chest as he kisses her cheek, wiping away the tears streaming down her face.

"I look back over my shoulder when we've cleared a fence and saw the man still standing on the porch, calling out to me, 'Run, they're coming.'

Grace paused, laying quietly in Griff's arms then suddenly heaved a loud sigh and cried out. "It was my father. My father warned me they were coming."

"Who was coming, Grace?" Reece asked. "Who was he warning you about?"

"The Bannisters," she whispered. "When I looked back, I saw Luther Bannister walk around the side of the house and shoot my father. Lamont and Luke followed on horses. My father fell back against the door, in pain, He was strong though and still able to stand when Luther approached him. He pushed my father back into the flames of the burning house."

"You were lucky to escape," Reece said. "Your father loved you and he died trying to protect you. No one can ask any more of a man. I can't say my father would have done the same for me."

The three sat together on the rocky hill. Grace's muffled crying finally subsided and she drank from the canteen Reece offered. She was exhausted and wanted to go home. The morning had been tedious and she wanted nothing more but to go back to the Emerald and never see this desolate place again.

"How did you end up here on foot, Grace?" Griff, said, finally breaking the silence.

"I'm not sure. I remember riding hard, too frightened to look back to see if I was being followed. I must have stopped by water and rested. I remember trees nearby. They always appear in my dreams so it must be important. As for anything else, I have no idea how I ended up on foot." She drew a deep breath and sighed. "I'm afraid I still don't know what the Bannisters were after or why they wanted my father dead."

"They wanted you both dead," said Reece. "That fact hasn't escaped me."

"Maybe it's a secret lost with them. The saddlebags must be important. Why else would I dream about them so much?"

"What about John Cooper?" Griff asked. He glanced at Reece then back to Grace. "Any recollection of your former fiancé? What he looked like. His associations. I was wondering if you thought he knew the Bannisters."

"Griffin, what are you asking?" said Grace, shocked at the idea. "Surely you aren't suggesting that I would agree to marry a man who was involved with those men. They killed my father. I doubt he knew the Bannisters."

"I say we're done with questions for the day." Reece said. "Its been a long morning and we're all tired. We've learned a great deal and when I get back to town I can send a letter to the marshal in Carson City. Maybe he knows of a ranch that was burned." He lightly squeezed Grace's shoulders. "You did well, today. Now we have more information."

"Reece is right," said Griff. "I'll bet Jesse is working himself into a lather just worrying about us. We ought to make it back to the Emerald about lunch time."

He knew it might be a mistake to bring up John Cooper but Grace remembered so much Griff was hoping she might still have a few more answers. If Reece was correct, the man would appear in her dreams as others had. If he didn't, then perhaps Will Spencer had news from San Francisco.

Jesse did not ask about the trip to the hills when the three returned. Grace knew his pride would not allow it after his comments to Reece when they left that morning. She hugged him after dismounting then handed over the reins of her horse. She would repeat her story for him later. The others did not realize that, along with the flashbacks of her father's death, came the memories of his life. Each mile of the path home brought a clearer vision of this man who had warned her of danger. He had been the voice in her dreams whispering caution. The voice she had never forgotten even though she, for a time, had not remembered him.

She sat on the bed looking at the contents of the saddlebag. Their significance was now clear. Her father must have known the Bannisters would come and prepared for her escape. Grace recognized the portrait, now. It was indeed her mother who had been killed when she was younger. A wagon she was riding in overturned after its team of horses were spooked and ran wild. The comb was a childhood gift from her father. The cameo belonged to her grandmother, an immigrant from England. It was a gift from a young British naval officer who pledged his love only to be lost at sea. Her grandmother mourned the loss of the young man throughout her life or so was the story passed down from her mother. She cherished these things more than ever now that she knew their history.

"Everything alright, Gracie?" Jesse had opened the door a crack in hopes of finding her still awake. She was surprised that it was him and not Griffin who had come to check on her.

"Yes, Jesse, come in."

I owe you an apology for the way I acted this morning," he said, patting her leg as he sat on the edge of the bed. "Reece and Griffin are fine young men but sometimes young men don't realize how delicate the feelings of a young woman can be. Reece is a good sheriff who is dedicated to his job, although sometimes maybe too dedicated. Griff loves you and only wants to see you happy."

"You know he loves me?" Grace asked wide-eyed. "It seems everyone has guessed."

"Of course, I know," Jesse said, laughing. "You forget, I've known that boy since the day he was born. I can sense with every twitch, every outburst and every smile what he's feeling. Heck, I know what he's thinking before he does."

Grace blushed as Jesse spoke. It seemed like everyone in the county had realized Griffin's love for her and yet he had never expressed his feelings. "He's never told me he cared. I'm embarrassed to admit I wasn't sure until Elizabeth mentioned something at the barbeque. I have even given some thought as to what I might do when my memory comes back. If perhaps I should try to build my own life or move away."

"Listen here, little miss. You're not going anywhere. You love him and he loves you. In fact, the whole family loves you, me included. Why, Tom got to blubbering the other day about how Eleanor would have loved you just as much as Elizabeth and he will be proud to have you as part of his family. Of course, every time Tom has a little too much whiskey he starts blubbering." Jesse cleared his throat and paused, regretting his comment.

"I love all of you too," Grace said, as her eyes began to well with tears. "Rachel is like a sister and I think Elizabeth would be too." She looked down for a moment as she spoke. "I guess Tom isn't the only one who blubbers."

"You're going to stay right here on the Emerald with us. You'll be married and have a family and make a cranky old man happy by providing a few babies to rock in my old age."

"Jesse," Grace exclaimed, her face turning red once again.

He leaned over and kissed her forehead then started for the door. "You get some sleep and I'll have no more talk about you leaving."

She dimmed the lamp and settled under the quilt. Like an old friend, it comforted and kept her safe as she slept. She was drained from the events of the day and needed sleep. Once more, the trip to the hills and the recollections of her life seeped into her thoughts. So much had come back to her and so much more would, she was sure. She would not go to Denver to speak with Allister Neal. She hoped she never heard the name Bannister again and John Cooper was a man best left in the past. She would tell Griffin tomorrow that she did not want him or Reece to pursue occurrences which were over now. She would also tell him her most treasured news. She had remembered her name. She was no longer Grace, the lost girl from the hills. She was Anne Bedford.

CHAPTER 14

The Girl from Rosehill

Griffin sipped the hot coffee as he sat on the front porch. He had tossed and turned all night, going over details which emerged from Grace's memories after their trip to the hills. She had finally gotten closure by remembering her parents and the ranch where she grew up. Sad as it was for her, it was as much of a relief for him as it was her. With the discovery of her identity, came the promise that they could move on with their lives. Still, he was unsettled. Although, he felt that once again she was safe, there were events not yet remembered. He wanted to put those to rest as well, lest they raise their ugly head again later.

He thought it unlikely that Grace or her father were involved in John Cooper's cattle rustling schemes but he could not forget that the Bannisters had killed her father and were willing to kill Grace as well. He and Reece knew that Cooper was a criminal and a person to be reckoned with. Was it he that ordered them killed? Was Grace a target because she had witnessed her father's death or did she have knowledge of what they were after. Why else would the Bannisters hound her to the point of their own extinction? Grace's few belongings had been recovered without containing a hint of anything valuable. They had both looked over the contents of the saddle bag numerous times and there was nothing of value. He believed her dreams were the key to the answer but moaned in misery at the thought of those vague hints continuing to invade her sleep. These questions kept him up most of the night until, finally giving up on sleep, he had gotten up, made a pot of coffee and now sat watching a glorious sunrise.

He took another sip of coffee, wondering if it wasn't time to stoke the fire in the stove. He was getting hungry and saw a light flickering in Jesse's room in the barn. A rider appeared on the path from the road and he recognized Reece as he got closer to the house.

"Don't you have some place else to go for breakfast? I'm going to have to start billing the sheriff's office for your meals," Griff said as his friend climbed the porch steps and sat down.

"It sure isn't your fine hospitality that brings me here. Got any more of that coffee?"

"Inside, but keep quiet. Grace is still sleeping."

Reece stepped inside and returned moments later with the coffee pot, pouring himself a large cup and refilling Griff's. "Something bothering you or have you decided to take up homestead in that chair? I would think a man with a ranch to run would have better things to do."

"I'd be willing to guess that whatever is bothering me is the same thing that brought you here so early," Griff answered. "You have any news for me?"

"I had a message from the sheriff in a town west of Sweetwater."

"Over by the state border?" Griff asked. Reece nodded in agreement.

"There's a small ranch called Rosehill not too far from the town. The sheriff says the house and barn were burned to the ground and two people killed. A man and his daughter were inside when the fire started. They buried what was left of the man but never found the daughter. He figures the fire was so hot there was just nothing left of her body. The man's name was James Bedford. The daughter's name was Anne."

"What are you saying? Is this daughter supposed to be Grace, because she is inside, asleep?" Griff was skeptical of Reece's explanation.

"If you let me finish, I was about to get to that. You see, up until a couple of days ago, the sheriff thought Anne Bedford was dead. He never paid attention to all the previous inquires I sent. In his mind, he didn't have a missing woman in his town. He only had a dead one who had been killed in a fire. It wasn't until he got my last message asking about John Cooper that he started to put it all together. The horse, saddle and her saddlebag with the Rosehill brand on them. I think he's a little embarrassed it took him so long to figure it out. According to him, by the time they got to the ranch, everything was burned to the ground and the horses and cattle were gone."

"What about the Bannisters? Did it ever occur to him that they might be involved?" Griff said. "Didn't he think it odd that the animals were missing? It doesn't sound like he did a lot of investigating. I'm wondering if the sheriff took the time to search for those responsible for the fire and murders. Or did it occur to him that it might be murder? "

"It occurred to him and he suspected the Bannisters involvement. He also thought they were connected to John Cooper.

James Bedford complained to the sheriff that he and other ranchers were being pressured to sell out by a group of investors from Denver but they refused."

"Does it strike you as a coincidence that Denver keeps popping up everywhere we turn?"

"Denver, Cooper, Grace's saddle, it's all tied together. I should have gone to Denver like I planned," said Reece.

"You were right to take her to the hills first. We wouldn't know as much about her father's death if we hadn't. It did her good to remember. What else did this sheriff say?"

"Like I said, the ranchers are being pressured to sell and one day this John Cooper shows up in town. He's a fancy dressed, smart talking gentleman, claiming to be from California. Cooper tells Bedford he has a way to turn his 400 acres into a goldmine by helping to move cattle. He paints this rosy picture of how, together, they will make a fortune and then starts courting Bedford's daughter."

"You mean Anne."

"The sheriff was suspicious of John Cooper from the beginning but Bedford is taken in by Cooper's talk. The sheriff has heard the tales from the cattleman's association about moving stolen cattle but he didn't have any evidence that Cooper was involved. He just had to sit back and wait. He did, however, make Bedford aware of the cattle rustling scheme which could be in the works."

"Did Grace's father ever figure out that John Cooper was involved?" asked Griff.

"The sheriff thinks he did. Apparently, Cooper starts telling everyone in town that he's engaged to Grace...I mean Anne. Seems like no one in town ever remembers those words coming out of her mouth, though. She didn't even seem to be too fond of him at all. Things start to fall apart when Bannister's oldest son, Luke, shows up in town one night. He gets drunk and spills the beans to some saloon girl about how he is going to run the Rosehill ranch and become a big cattle investor like John Cooper. The saloon girl doesn't like the way Luke Bannister is talking because she knows the Bedfords to be honest people, so she repeats the story to the sheriff who takes a ride out to Rosehill and tells James Bedford. The next thing he knows, Bedford is dead, his ranch burned and Cooper nowhere to be found."

"So, the sheriff's theory is that Bedford realizes Cooper is a crook and confronts him. Cooper decides to have him killed so he doesn't ruin his plans."

"Exactly. By the time the sheriff finds Bedford dead, Cooper has skipped town. The strange part is that Cooper sent the sheriff a letter, later, claiming that Bedford had already agreed to sell the ranch to him and since he was Anne's fiancé and she was also dead, it rightfully belonged to him."

"Don't tell me. He sent the letter from Denver."

Reece holds up his hand signaling Griff to keep quiet. "Let me finish. Cooper's letter says it was the way Anne and her father would have wanted it."

"If Cooper wasn't guilty of something then why did he leave town? If he and Anne were engaged, why not stay and give the Bedfords a proper funeral. It all sounds like a tall tale to me," Griff said trying to follow along.

"It sounded like a tall take to the sheriff also. He didn't buy the story that Bedford was going to sell to Cooper. Bedford never had any intentions of selling out. The sheriff didn't believe Cooper had ever cared for Anne at all. He got a judge to put a hold on any change in ownership of that ranch until an investigation was completed and a deed could be produced. He was hoping it would buy him some time."

"I suppose Cooper showed up with the deed and took the ranch," Griff said, pouring more coffee.

"That's the thing. Cooper sent the letter, then disappeared. He hasn't contacted the sheriff or anyone else and no one knows where the deed to the Bedford ranch is."

"Do you think John Cooper is dead?" Griff asked. "Maybe the Bannisters double crossed him."

"I've known people to double cross someone for less but, no, I don't think he's dead. I think he's looking for the deed and I believe that's what the Bannisters were after. The Bannisters were supposed to get rid of James and Anne Bedford but they let Anne slip through their fingers.

"Mr. Bedford knew the Bannisters were coming for him, didn't he? That's why he had Anne packed and ready to go and why he warned her when they were coming," said Griff. "He had to have known at that point that she would also be killed if she stayed."

"But the Bannisters followed Anne and thought they had killed her up in the hills," said Reece. "They would have too if you hadn't gone hunting for a cougar. Thinking she was dead probably prompted Cooper to write that letter to the sheriff declaring his right to the ranch.

Cooper finds out Anne is still alive and lays low until the Bannisters have time to come back here to finish the job. They needed to recover the deed. If Cooper gets his hands on the deed, he can claim ownership and there is nothing the law can do about it. Anne will lose her home and he's free to resume his cattle rustling scheme."

Griff shot straight up in his chair looking at Reece. "You think her father sent her off with the deed to protect her and their ranch?"

"That's exactly what I think," Reece answered. "It's why the Bannisters were looking for her horse and saddle. They might have thought the deed was hidden in the saddle some place. We're just lucky the miner didn't sell the saddlebag."

"If Grace doesn't have the deed then where do you suppose it is?"

Well, I've been thinking about that too. Grace lived west of Sweetwater but when she rides off from her ranch after her father is killed, she rides east, heading this way."

"Correct," said Griffin. "And she ends up in the hills. I'm not seeing your point."

Then it's a good thing I'm the sheriff and you're not," Reece said in an exasperated voice. "What is the one thing that consistently happens in her dreams?"

"The same thing over and over. She's riding the horse and stops by water and remembers trees..." Griff paused midsentence and smiled at Reece then continues in an excited voice. "And if I am traveling east from Sweetwater, the only stream next to a grove of trees is that place where you and me and Matt stopped on our hunting trip. The stream where we went fishing. By the cliffs."

"I always wondered why the Bannisters left the church social and went up into the hills where they had been camped for days, then broke camp and turned west. It's not that unusual that they would want to skedaddle out of there but why not head north through the hills? It would have been a safer path of escape and more difficult to track them. How did they come to end up hiding in those cliffs by that stream?"

"Because they were looking for the deed," Griffin cried out, slapping his leg as he realized what Reece was trying to say. "She hid the deed by the stream or those trees or in the cliffs somewhere. That's why she keeps having the dream. It's been right there in front of us the whole time, we just didn't know what it meant."

"We couldn't have known what it meant. We had to let it play out and now it has," Reece said, still grinning. "Grace always knew the answers to her own mystery. She just needed to separate the fog to see them."

"What do you want to do now?" Griffin asked.

"First, I'd like some breakfast. I've been up half the night turning this stuff over in my mind and I'm starved. After that, I think you and I need to take a little ride over to that stream and look around a bit. Just you and me, I don't want to involve Grace until we see if we can find this on our own. Once again, I think its best if she sticks close to the ranch until we know who else might still be hunting for that deed."

"Where do you think Cooper is now? The last person to see him alive was Allister Neal, the gentleman who bought the saddle," Griff said.

"I wish I knew."

"Griffin, what are you two doing out on the porch this early?" Grace was standing in the doorway. She brushed back her hair with one hand while tightly holding her robe closed at the neck with the other. "You woke me with all your shouting."

Both men jumped up and stood at attention like school boys who were caught engineering a prank on a fellow student. "I'm sorry. Reece happened to come by. Missing your good cooking, I guess. Seems you spoiled him when he was staying here."

"I just stopped by to express my thanks again for taking such good care of me when I was down and out. You know how Griff is always telling wild stories. I could not get him to quiet down."

Grace took a deep breath and shook her head. "I don't know what you two are up to but whatever it is, I know you can't do it on an empty stomach. If you want eggs you're going to have to fetch them from the coop yourself and I'll need more firewood. Where's my coffee pot?"

⅄

Reece stood talking to Jesse while Griffin lingered on the porch with Grace. She packed left over biscuits and ham from breakfast and looked with wondering eyes as Griff explained their sudden urge to travel west, helping Reece track down a couple of outlaws he'd been chasing. Griff hated to lie to Grace but he thought it best if they didn't reveal the information they received from the Sweetwater sheriff. Anyway, it wasn't really a lie. They were indeed tracking outlaws. He had just not mentioned they were the outlaws associated with her father's death.

"I still don't know why you have to go with him," Grace said, sensing something was not right with their story. "Do you always spend this much time helping Reece with his sheriff duties? I thought that was Deputy Vance's job."

"See that's the thing, Grace," Griff said. "Deputy Vance is still recovering from his injuries and can't ride. You know Reece is a good friend and I need to help him with this."

"When will you be back? I was hoping you would take me to town this afternoon. You two have practically run me out of coffee and flour and there were a few other things I needed."

"I'll be back this afternoon. Jesse can take you to town, then when I get back we can go on that picnic I've been promising. I've got a little spot all picked out for us. There is something I want to tell you. There are a lot of things I want to tell you. One thing special I'd like to say."

Grace smiled as she reached up and combed her fingers through his sandy hair. "There are some things I'd like to say to you too. I'll make a big lunch because I know you'll be hungry. You'll be careful, won't you?"

"I'll be especially careful, just for you. Don't worry, Grace. You and I are going to be just fine." He bent down to kiss her and held her for a moment then climbed down the stairs and on to his horse.

Grace stood watching as they left and waved to Griffin when he looked back at her before the two men disappeared down the road. There was work for her to do if she were to go on a picnic. Morning chores were finished quickly fueled by Grace's desire to have everything in order when Griffin got back. They were going on a picnic she kept repeating and he had something to tell her. He said he had picked out a spot for them and that made her smile. Since Reece had shown up early that morning, they had no time to be alone so she had not told Griff she remembered her name. She would wait until their picnic.

Grace's daydreams were interrupted when she heard horses pull up and was delighted to see Rachel step down from her buggy. She wanted to tell her about the picnic. Wanted her to know about her new memories. With her original plans to go to Denver, herself, she thought she might never see her friend again. Now, she would stay at the Emerald and they might be family in the future.

"Is everything alright out here with you two?" Rachel asked as she gave Grace a hug. "You acted a little odd at the barbeque. I hope you and Griff didn't have an argument. I've been a little worried. Remember he loves you."

If one more person says that, Grace thought, I'm going to scream. She looked forward to the picnic even more than she had before. She desperately wanted to speak to Griff about her feelings and hopefully hear him confess the same for her.

"Things are wonderful," Grace replied, smiling. "Although, yesterday it wasn't quite that nice. Reece and Griffin and I went back up to the hills. I have to say, it was frightening but I have regained so much of my memory, including my name which is actually Anne Bedford."

"Anne Bedford, isn't that strange," remarked Rachel. She paused for a moment realizing what she had said and laughed nervously. "I don't mean your name is strange. Just that, I happened to be in town yesterday having lunch with Margaret. She wants the three of us to get together. She's grown fond of you. She also wants to make plans for the garden party tea. I told her Elizabeth and I talked to you in to it. I hope that's alright that I took the liberty to say so. You'll come, won't you? It will be fun for the three of us. Wait, there would be four because Elizabeth wants to be included. Anyway, Margaret and I ate lunch in the hotel which we generally don't do but there was something I wanted to pick up at Miller's and we were right there so it made sense to eat at the hotel first..."

Grace listened with patience as Rachel described her lunch and just about every dress offered for sale at Miller Mercantile. She was always fascinated with the way Griff's sister could produce an endless stream of words in relaying a story without really having said much by the time she was through. It was an endearing feature and made her feel comfortable to be around someone who was always so excited about everything in life.

"Where is Griffin, anyway?" Rachel finally asked. "I saw Jesse riding through the pasture when I came up the road but didn't see Griff with him."

"He and Reece have gone off in search of a clue about outlaws. Evidently Reece has been trying to find these fellows and Deputy Vance is laid up with his bad leg so Griff went along to help. I hope Jesse isn't gone all day. He is supposed to take me into town."

"I can take you," Rachel said. "Actually, that's why I came to see you. As I started to say, Margaret and I had lunch at the hotel and as we were leaving, a man approached me and asked if I knew Anne Bedford. Of course, I said no and that I had never heard of anyone by that name around here. He corrected himself and said he believed the woman was currently using the name Grace and might be staying at the Emerald ranch."

"Who was this man?" asked Grace with curiosity. "Why would someone be asking about Anne Bedford when I just yesterday figured out that was my real name. That is strange, indeed."

"I thought so too," answered Rachel. "I thought it was important and of course I was surprised when he said that this Anne Bedford went by the name Grace. Of course, I had no idea at the time. You can imagine how surprised this gentleman was when he found out that I was Griff's sister and that I knew you and the Emerald very well. I told him you had been staying here since you were found in the hills almost dead and lost your memory."

"What did he want?"

"He is an associate of a man named Allister Neal whose name sounded familiar but I couldn't place it at the time. Lance reminded me that he was the gentleman you purchased your saddle from."

"Allister Neal," Grace said with surprise. "I planned to go to Denver to visit with him. I was hoping he might have information that could lead me to John Cooper but I've since changed my mind. How does he come to be in town?"

"On business or something," answered Rachel. "Mr. Neal knew that Griffin had purchased the saddle and was traveling in the area and wanted to look him up to make sure he was happy with it. He asked if you would be willing to meet with him briefly today."

Grace thought for a moment. She did want to meet with Allister Neal and this was working out perfectly that he should be in town. She hesitated to go alone and wondered if she shouldn't send word back with Rachel that she and Griffin would be happy to meet with him tomorrow.

"I'm afraid Griff wouldn't like it if I went by myself. He and Reece asked that I stay close to the ranch until they get back and we have a picnic planned," she said.

"He is too protective. Honestly, he acts like you might break into a million pieces if left alone. I'll take you. That way we don't have to interrupt Jesse's work and it will be fun for the two of us to go to town. We can stop by and see Margaret while we're there. She'll love it and Griff certainly can't get angry because you are not alone. You have me to protect you."

Maybe you're right, said Grace. "I wouldn't actually be going alone and I really did need to pick up some things. We could go to town, see Margaret, meet with Mr. Neal and be back in time for the picnic. Give me a few minutes to get ready."

She went to the bedroom and quickly dressed. Opening the drawer of the nightstand, she pulled out the cameo brooch belonging to her grandmother and pinned it over the top button of her dress. It would bring her good luck in her quest to find out more information. She looked at the pistol Griff had stored in the drawer. He told her it would always be there to protect her if she needed. He would be proud of her for remembering to take it. It was her first adventure away from the Emerald without him. She could finally prove her independence. Placing the gun in her bag, she walked out to meet Rachel.

"You look wonderful," Rachel exclaimed. "You must let me borrow that dress but only if it looks as good on me as it does on you."

Grace scribbled a quick note for Jesse, letting him know where she had gone then joined Rachel in the buggy. Her stomach was full of flutters from the excitement of going to town and spending time with her friend. It was going to be a wonderful outing and she would be home before anyone realized she was gone.

CHAPTER 15

Treasure Revealed

Griff climbed down from his saddle and stretched his legs. The small stream and grove of trees were a familiar sight and never seemed like a large area until now when they needed to search for something so small. The cliffs, where the Bannisters made their stand a few weeks before, were steep but not especially high. The memories of his struggle to climb to the top as rocks crumbled under his feet and bullets ricocheted around him, made the jagged crag seem more ominous. He wondered how more of the men who rode with Reece that day hadn't been injured or killed.

Reece stared at the cliffs, too. Griff was sure his friend carried his own memories of the day when he lay on the ground wounded, struggling to remain conscious as others continued the fight with the Bannisters.

Chet Larson, was a skilled surgeon in the war, and experienced in temporarily patching wounded soldiers. He used that experience then to bandage Tom Kelly, Deputy Vance, Reece and the others. It was too late to save Luther and his son, Luke. The ground where those men were carried was still stained with their blood.

When Griff and Lance reached the scene that afternoon of the gunfight, their father's health was a priority. Lance helped Doctor Larson prepare to transport Tom and the others to a place of safety where he could provide further treatment. Griff sat down beside his friend.

"'Bout time you got here," Reece complained as Griff placed a blanket under his head."

"You told me to stay, remember? I knew you'd need my help," Griff replied, offering Reece water from his canteen. "You're not looking too good right now."

"I'll be fine," Reece breathlessly replied, wincing when Griff pulled back the bandages from his side, revealing torn flesh from a bullet wound. "How's Tom?"

"He's in pain. Doc put a tourniquet on. He's going to take you both home. We already loaded Vance in the wagon."

"I'll wait for the rest of you" said Reece. "This was my idea. I'll see it through to the end."

"No, it was my idea. I pushed you to follow these guys. You said yourself, last night, it was dangerous and the men in the posse were your responsibility. I shouldn't have talked you into it."

"You didn't talk me into it." Reece held his side, moaning as he awkwardly tried to sit up. "I never let you talk me into anything. I've known what I was doing this whole time."

"Then how did you get yourself shot?"

"Are you two squabbling?" The sound of Tom Kelly's irate voice, reverberated above noise of gunfire. "With all of this going on? Put Reece in the wagon so we can go home and get this bullet out of my leg."

"We're just talking, Pa."

"Tell your pa, I'm staying." Reece, laid back down and tried to find a comfortable spot on the ground below him.

"Once again, leave me to clean up." Griff looked at the bloody hole in Reece's side once more then covered his chest again with the bandages. "You've taken women uglier than that wound to the church social. Hang on 'til I get back."

He squeezed Reece's arm and placed his canteen near the sheriff's hand then pulled his gun from the holster. "Lance and I will finish this, so stay put if you want and don't give the doc any trouble while I'm gone." Motioning for Lance to follow, they both walked toward the cliffs and the sound of continued gun fire.

"Reece?"

"Huh?"

"You alright? I just asked where you wanted to start looking," Griff said, interrupting Reece's thoughts. They walked to the stream, leading the horses. The sun was growing hot and they knelt to drink from the cool water.

"The way I see it, if the Bannisters were following Grace then she would have wanted to hide the deed as quickly as possible. She probably didn't have much time. I doubt she would have started up those rocks."

"This may have been where she lost her horse," said Griff. "In the dreams, the horse is always here by the water. The Bannisters could have surprised her when she stopped. She didn't have a lot of resources to use. No gun to defend herself. I don't think she had any choice but to run."

"If that's true, it would have been a heck of a long way to the hills on foot. No wonder she was exhausted."

"I'm surprised she made it that far. Her will to survive was strong. You think she hid the deed near the stream or the trees?" said Griff. "I vote for the trees."

"No telling. You start with them and I'll walk the bank."

Griff headed toward the trees, looking at the ground for anything unusual. His eyes moved back and forth hoping to spot a patch of displaced dirt or grass. He kicked around the trunk of each tree and brushed back leaves accumulated under fallen branches. Moss on the side of one trunk had been scraped away and that seemed encouraging but it was the only hint of anything out of the ordinary. Maybe she dug a hole some place, he thought.

He looked out to the stream where Reece walked, pausing occasionally to turn over a rock or push away the dense growth of cattails, clustered along the shore. Griff glanced at the low-lying branches and moved behind a tree. She would have been concealed from the Bannisters momentarily in the protection of the trees, he thought. Could have been long enough to hide something. He glanced around again but saw nothing of interest.

"This is going to be impossible," he grumbled. "We haven't the first idea where she's hidden it." Frustrated, he sat down on a log and waited for Reece, trying to think of what he would do if he had been in Grace's shoes that day. Where would he hide something if he was being chased and had little time?

Satisfied there was nothing hidden close to the water, Reece joined him. "Do you think the deed is here or are we just wasting our time? Maybe we guessed wrong about her dreams," Griff said.

"It's here," Reece answered scanning the landscape. "You need some patience. It's not going to jump out at us. Let's look around some more and if we can't find anything then I suggest we bring Grace over. She seems to remember best when she's put in the actual setting where an event occurred. We might have gone about this the wrong way by not including her from the start. It could be the only way."

"If we do that, then I want to wait a couple of days. I've been promising to take her on a picnic. There are some things we need to talk about. Who knows, maybe after we spend some time alone it will no longer be important to her."

Reece slapped Griff on the back as he stood. "You just keep thinking that. I believe I'll spend a little time over by the cliffs. I may climb up a piece. Could be, she did take the time to hide it up in those rocks."

Griffin watched as his friend walked toward the rocky cliffs thinking of Grace. He lowered his head and went over the words he would use when he told her he loved her. A shiny object peeked out through the dirt below his feet and he dug at the ground to loosen it.

Nothing but an old pocket knife, he thought. It's probably been here forever. The blade is starting to rust. He tossed it to the side and stared at the rotting bark of the old log he was perched on. It tore away easily as he picked at it, revealing the smooth surface underneath. Something struck him as odd when he caught sight of a small shape scratched into the surface. It was barely visible, almost blending into the wood. He studied the image for a moment, running his finger over the small indentation, making sure his eyes were not deceiving him and a slow grin formed on his face. The small shallow carving, hastily created, was shaped like a crescent moon.

That was the description Grace used when describing the dream where Lamont first appeared. The young boy shouted to her in that dream, his words resonating now. Find the moon he had urged. This old log, where she had hidden that precious object, now revealed its treasure. She must have scratched the moon shape into the wood with that old knife.

Griff rolled the old log over. There, underneath, was a small layer of twigs and brushing them to the side he saw a mound of dirt ten inches long and six inches wide indicating someone had recently dug a hole and hurriedly covered it again. He clawed frantically at the area with his fingers, moving the dirt out until he felt something buried underneath. Picking up the knife he had thrown aside, he stabbed at the earth to soften the spot, pushing away chunks of wet, soft earth until he uncovered a bound piece of rawhide. Opening it carefully he saw the deed.

The last piece of the puzzle was complete. He sighed with relief, smiling as he thought of the job he and Reece had done in pursuing the answer to this mystery. They could go back to the Emerald and show Grace the paper she risked her life to preserve. He tucked the small knife into his pocket and rose then stopped suddenly when he heard a click as the hammer of a gun was pulled back.

"Turn around real slow and don't reach for your gun or I'll shoot you dead before your hand touches the holster."

Griffin did as he was told and found himself facing Lamont Bannister. He was hardly recognizable and in obvious pain from the bandaged right thigh. The smell told Griff that gangrene had set in. His clothes were filthy. One side of his face caked with dirt and blood. His eyes sunken, bordered by dark circles. It was apparent he hadn't slept and Griff suspected the battered man hadn't eaten much either. Bannister was weak but that did not stop him from pointing the Colt 45 at Griff's chest.

"Drop your gun on the ground and throw that rawhide over here," Lamont said wincing as he spoke.

Again, Griff did as he was told, letting his gun fall and tossing the wrapped deed at Lamont's feet. He quickly glanced toward the cliffs then stared at the outlaw.

"Are you that Emerald man they talk about? The one who's been taking care of her?" Lamont glared with hatred in his eyes.

"I'm afraid I don't know what you're talking about. I just came out here to do a little fishing. If you don't mind, I'll be getting back to it."

"You know who I mean. Anne Bedford, the woman you found in the hills. People say you saved her life."

"She said the same thing about you," Griff replied. "Once she got her memory back and could recall how you and your family left her for dead. What kind of a man would leave a woman to die in those hills? Now, why don't you put that gun down and I'll be happy to discuss this with you."

"I had no choice. She was a witness and my pa wanted her gone. You think I wanted to kill her? I did what I could to save her. I've cared about Anne since we were kids." Lamont waved his gun at Griff. "Move back."

"She was always nice to me when we were young and my pa and brother, Luke, worked for her father. Heck, I taught her how to shoot. We would ride together sometimes. She'd have to sneak off when her pa wasn't looking because I was a Bannister and not good enough for his precious Anne."

"Your pa worked for her father?" Griff asked

"Many years ago. Then Mr. Bedford caught him and Luke stealing his cattle and fired them. He told the sheriff and they would have been arrested, probably even hanged if they hadn't gone to Denver and met up with John Cooper. My pa hated Bedford after that and vowed revenge. Cooper helped him get it."

"By trying to force Anne's father to sell or by rustling more cattle from him or was it by just plain killing him?"

"I'd say it was all three. Cooper ran his operation out of Denver and still does. He knew my pa was familiar with Rosehill and could easily move the cattle. That's why he wanted the ranch. Cooper sent Bedford a letter under a different name and offered to buy him out, but he refused. Mr. Bedford had never met John Cooper. They only corresponded by mail. When he showed up in town, Anne's pa never put things together. He tried again to buy Rosehill and when that didn't work decided he would marry Anne, then get rid of her father. Once Bedford was dead, Cooper could just as easily get rid of Anne, leaving us to run the business. But Cooper was mistaken. Anne had no interest in marrying him. He had to think of something else.

It was my family's job to force Mr. Bedford to turn over the deed or kill him if need be. Of course, we had to make it look like an accident. In return, we would get full control of the Rosehill and be free to run the stolen cattle out of the Bedford ranch. For a sizable share of the profits, I might add. Once Cooper got his hands on that deed, he didn't need Anne anymore and she was to face her own accidental death. I hated the idea from the beginning but there was no talking my pa out of it. Cooper created another letter claiming he had called off the engagement. He instructed my pa to make Anne's death look like a suicide. The letter was to be found on her body so people would think she died of a broken heart. He made the whole thing up.

"How did Anne come into possession of the letter? If we hadn't found it in her saddlebag we never would have known about John Cooper," Griff asked.

"I don't know but somehow she got a hold of it and that's what warned her father that something was up. Bedford knew we were coming for him that day. I think my drunken brother must have talked too much around town. When we got to the house, he was waiting. We weren't expecting Anne to be there. We threw torches into the house to start the fire and figured to shoot them when they ran out. Bedford wasn't about to let that happen. He holed up with a rifle, shooting back at us. That left time for Anne to escape out the back door. We didn't realize it, until she was already mounted and riding off. That set my pa on the chase. He wasn't about to be shown up by some puny woman. He had no intentions of letting her live. I tried to stop him when we ran her down in those hills but he wouldn't hear of it. The best I could do was to lie. That's why I told her not to move. It was the only way for her to survive. Then Luke said he'd seen her in town. I had to know for myself that she was still alive so I snuck out to your ranch and watched her hanging the laundry. I didn't mean to scare her, I promise. I never meant her any harm."

"She's healthy now and will be able to identify you in court."

"She'll never get the chance. I'm taking this deed back to John Cooper, collect my money and leaving the state."

"Anne told us the story of how your pa killed her father and how she got away," Griff said. "Didn't work out too well for your pa, did it? He's the one that ended up dead. What do you say we make a deal?"

"What kind of deal do you think I'd make with you?" Lamont, spit at Griff then wiped his mouth on his sleeve. "No, Emerald man. I got no reason to make a deal with you."

Griff ignored Lamont, suspecting he was growing weaker and hoped to stall for time. He looked at the cliffs again, then back at Bannister. "You let me have the deed and I'll let you go peacefully. I'll give you a head start. Bet you'll be half way to California before I can even notify Sheriff Cameron. That's a pretty good offer, Bannister."

"How about I take the deed and in exchange for your cooperation, I won't kill you? John Cooper is willing to pay me a lot of money for this piece of paper. Rosehill is a prime piece of land and he wants it bad."

"I'm afraid I can't let you do that Lamont," said a voice from behind. "Put the gun down."

Lamont spun around to find Reece with his gun pointed at him. "We've been looking for you and your family for a long time. It's pretty satisfying to finally come face to face with the surviving Bannister. Now, put down that gun. You're under arrest for the murder of James Bedford."

"Damn you to hell, sheriff," Lamont shouted. He poised to shoot when Griff dove to the ground and grabbed his gun. There was a sound of gunfire and Lamont Bannister fell to the ground. Stunned, he raised his gun once more and aimed at the sheriff. Reece fired back.

Lamont lay writhing in pain as Griff and Reece knelt beside him. His breathing was labored as he held his side, blood oozing from the wound. "I never meant for Anne to get hurt. I tried to protect her."

"I believe you did," Griff said. "Answer me one question. You told me John Cooper first corresponded with Anne's father using a different name. What was the name he used?"

Lamont looked at Griff with disdain. "You think I'd tell you? Find Allister Neal."

Griff threw a curious look at Reece and knew the sheriff was wondering the same thing. They were surprised that Lamont Bannister knew Allister Neal.

"What does Allister Neal have to do with all of this? Are you trying to tell me he's involved somehow?"

Lamont cried out in pain, his bloodied hand grabbing Griff's sleeve. He mustered one last chuckle as he stared at Griffin. "I guess you could say he's involved and he's come to town to meet up with Anne, today. He's going to kill her and none of us are going to be there to stop it."

"What are you talking about? Why does he want to harm Anne? What's she done to him?"

Lamont's hand relaxed and fell to his side. He closed his eyes. "You're a fool, Emerald man. Cooper uses many names in his business. It's how he's able to avoid the law. Haven't you figured it out, yet? Allister Neal is John Cooper."

CHAPTER 16

MEETING WITH MR. SMITH

"We've come for lunch," Rachel exclaimed when Margaret Spencer opened the door. "I hope you don't mind that we're unannounced but Grace and I were in town and knew you would be disappointed if we didn't stop by."

"You are so right, my dear." Margaret hugged both women then motioned them to come inside "You must have read my mind. I was telling Will this morning that I wanted all of us to get together. Where's Elizabeth? Didn't she come?"

"It's just the two of us," said Rachel. "I happened to be visiting Grace and she needed a few things in town so I offered to bring her."

"This is certainly a pleasant treat. I must say Grace, that look of happiness on your face is a wonderful sight to behold."

Grace blushed as she nervously uttered a thank you and stepped into the foyer, almost tripping over the large hall stand. She had never seen such a beautiful home and was embarrassed that she hadn't dressed more appropriately for their visit.

"Will was speaking with Griffin at the barbecue and of course he had such sweet things to say about you," Margaret went on, showing them into the parlor. "It's so nice you two have developed such a close friendship. I was about to have lunch but let's sit a moment then we'll eat by the garden in the back."

The Victorian-style house with its massive rooms and extensive wood trim seemed out of place in Nevada. Grace marveled at the beautiful woven rugs and decorated interior with its marble fireplace and European paintings.

A baby grand piano caught her attention. The long gold drapes hanging over the front windows made her feel as if she might be in a concert hall and she half expected to see a famous pianist enter and begin to play.

"I assume you have a trip to Miller Mercantile planned," said Margaret. "What's a trip to town unless you visit Miller's?"

"We're hoping to stop there before we leave but Grace has other business," Rachel answered. "She was asked to meet today with Allister Neal."

"Allister Neal," Margaret answered pensively. "Do I know him? I can't recall the name."

"Well, we don't really know him either. It's an interesting story and somewhat of a curious coincidence. You remember yesterday when we were having lunch at the hotel and the gentleman introduced himself? He is an acquaintance of Mr. Neal."

"Yes, I remember now. I thought it quite bold for a gentleman to invite a young lady to meet him at a hotel. It doesn't speak well of his manners, in my opinion."

"Margaret, I'm sure it was not a gesture meant to be anything improper. Besides there are two of us. What could happen?"

"Hmm, I don't like it Rachel. What business did you say he had with you, Grace? Do you think he's someone you may have known from your past?" Margaret was skeptical of this man and the meeting he proposed. With all that had happened to Grace, she questioned the wisdom for two women to meet with this gentleman with whom they weren't acquainted.

"He was the previous owner of my saddle," Grace answered. "Reece found Mr. Neal with the help of another sheriff. It was luck, I suppose. It seems he is in town for a short time and was hoping to meet briefly with Griff. There was a time when I thought of traveling to Denver to visit with him because he met my former fiancé briefly." Grace shrugged her shoulder, looking a little embarrassed at her explanation.

"I told you it was a coincidence," said Rachel. "For Allister Neal to happen to run into John Cooper is quite an opportunity for Grace."

"And why is Griffin not meeting with this Mr. Neal? Is he aware that you have an appointment?"

Grace looked at Rachel waiting for her to answer. She could see the look of consternation on Margaret's face and began to rethink her decision to come. "Well, Griffin left with Reece this morning to help with some sheriff duties. Something about looking for a clue to finding outlaws. Jesse was busy with the cattle and I really do need to pick up a few supplies."

"It worked out perfectly," Rachel added. "I just happened to stop by and it was convenient for me to bring her to town rather than having to wait for one of the men so, here we are."

"Yes, here you are," Margaret said still questioning the soundness of their plan.

"Besides," Rachel began again. "We aren't staying long. Griff is taking Grace on a picnic this afternoon so we need to get back. I thought it would be good for her to get out and naturally I wanted to bring her by to visit you."

"Well, I'm glad you did but I'm still worried about meeting with a man you've never seen. You don't know a thing about him. I'm afraid Tom wouldn't like it either. Why don't I send a message to

Will's office and ask him to accompany you both? I think that might be best."

"Oh, I wouldn't want to bother Mr. Spencer," Grace said. "I'm sure Mr. Neal is a gentleman and Rachel's right, it is an opportunity to have some of my questions about John Cooper answered. It means a great deal to me. I was hoping Mr. Neal could give me some information about how I might go about tracking him down. I don't think I'd bother if you two hadn't run into his assistant yesterday. Like I said, I had the idea to visit Mr. Neal in Denver at one time. I don't think Griff will mind. We won't stay long, of course."

"And when did you say Griffin would return? I'm sure he is anxious to meet Mr. Neal also."

"We'll be home long before Griff returns," said Rachel. "Did you say lunch was almost ready? If you like, we can always stop by after the meeting so you know things went well."

"Please do, I won't feel good about this until I hear from you. Let's go out on the patio. It's a beautiful day."

Margaret entertained the young women with stories of her early days in Nevada. She was raised in St. Louis and educated at a girl's school. It made sense to Grace that Margaret and Eleanor Kelly had an instant liking for each other and clung to their friendship in the early days when Nevada was still a territory. The Spencer's only child had died shortly after moving west making Eleanor's children important to Margaret.

"We really must go if we plan to get our shopping list taken care of," Rachel said. "I promise to bring Elizabeth with us next week and we can all have lunch at the hotel. I'll charge the bill to Pa."

"I'm sure you will, Rachel," laughed Margaret. She gave them both a hug. "Grace, I expect to see you and Griffin again soon."

"You will," smiled Grace as they left. She and Rachel climbed in the buggy and headed for the hotel.

"I hope we're doing the right thing, Rachel. I suddenly feel like this is a bad idea."

"Then we won't stay long. Just a quick hello, love the saddle, thanks so much and we'll head to the general store for your supplies. We're to meet them in the lobby."

Entering the hotel, they took a seat on a soft cushioned sofa, leaving a message at the desk for Mr. Smith, Allister Neal's assistant. It wasn't long before he approached them. Mr. Smith was a stocky, bald man of about fifty. He appeared nervous and continually grabbed at his pocket watch to check the time. He made little eye contact with the women and scanned the lobby suspiciously before leading them to a private dining room next to the hotel restaurant. Once there, he offered them a seat and asked them to wait.

"I really don't think this is a good idea, Rachel," Grace said, apprehensively. "I don't understand why Allister Neal didn't meet us in the lobby. Why do we have to sit back here in this little room? I think Margaret was right. This does not appear to be proper."

"I don't like it either. Mr. Smith seems too fidgety and it's starting to make me leery of this whole arrangement. I think we should just sneak out while no one is around. If Allister Neal wants to talk with you then he can go to the Emerald." Rachel sighed deeply and shot a worried look at Grace. "I'm sorry I got you into this mess."

"Don't worry about that now. Let's just worry about getting out of it."

The women crossed quietly to the other side of the room and gently turned the handle on the door. Pulling it open a couple of inches they saw Mr. Smith standing guard in front with his arms crossed and a pistol strapped to his hip. Rachel quickly closed the door again.

"Why is Mr. Smith standing guard at the door and where did that gun come from?" whispered Rachel. "He didn't have it when we walked in."

"I don't know but let's not stay around to find out. There's not another door in this room so we'll have to climb out the window."

They tiptoed to the window and peered out. It led to a side alley and would give them access to the main street. The alley was deserted so they could easily slip away unnoticed.

"I hope I don't tear my stockings crawling through this little opening," said Rachel as she struggled with the handle while Grace pushed up on the wood frame."

"Honestly, Rachel? Is that your biggest concern right now?"

A buildup of paint sealed the window and it would not budge. Grace searched the room for something heavy to throw through the glass but paused when the door opened and a man walked in followed by Mr. Smith.

"Well, well ladies. It hurts my feelings to see you trying to make such a hasty exit. Won't you please sit down?" The man motioned to the couch as Mr. Smith stood at the door with his hand on the handle of his gun.

The color drained from Grace's face and she grabbed Rachel's arm preventing her from moving. Frozen in place, she looked the man over, glaring when their eyes met. The man's sinister smile sickened her as he stood smugly staring back.

"John Cooper," she whispered in dismay as if he had risen from the dead.

"Hello, Anne or should I call you Grace? It's been quite a while, my sweet, and you seem to be causing me quite a few problems. I'm afraid your little adventure has to come to an end."

Rachel looked at Grace and then back again at the distinguished man who was now crossing the room toward them. "This is John Cooper? What happened to Allister Neal?"

"Why don't you sit down, Miss Kelly? This conversation is between me and Anne." He grabbed Rachel's arm, pulling her away from Grace and sending her toward the couch. She noticed Mr. Smith had now removed his gun from its holster and stood pointing it at her.

"What do you want, John? You and the Bannisters have already taken everything. What could I possibly have left that would be of value?"

"So, you do remember me," Cooper said as he glared at Grace. "I was under the impression that you had amnesia."

"I didn't remember until you walked in the door. Now, unfortunately, I have a flood of memories involving you and your attempt to take my father's ranch and see us both dead. What have you done with Allister Neal?"

"Oh, my dear Anne, I might have spared your life had you consented to marry me. I did have feelings for you. As far as Mr. Neal is concerned, that name is one of many I use when doing business. And that business for today is the whereabouts of the deed to the Bedford ranch. I have my men searching half the state looking for it."

"If you mean the Bannisters, they're dead," replied Grace with disdain.

Cooper stood towering over her as he drew closer, touching his body to hers. "It appears your devoted Lamont has survived and is prepared to bring me the deed by the end of the day. So, you see, it looks as if I have no further business with you. Too bad you brought along your friend. This is going to complicate things a bit. We're prepared to handle the death of an emotionally unstable young woman who was so grief stricken to learn of her father's death she took her own life. Now, I need to decide what to do with Miss Kelly. Unlike you, she will be missed."

"My father will kill you if you try to hurt either one of us," Rachel said.

"Your father is a boring old blowhard from what I understand and can't help you now. By the time he finds you, he won't recognize your face. What a shame, it's such a beautiful face."

"So, are you planning to shoot us right here? Aren't you afraid someone will hear?" Grace asked scanning the room for a makeshift weapon she could use to defend herself. She struggled to keep a clear head as Cooper paced back and forth in front of her and continued to threaten them.

"Oh, no that would be much too loud. We are all going for a walk through the door and out the side entrance of the hotel then down the alley right outside that window. At the end of the alley we'll find a wagon and you young ladies will be going for a ride. One you won't be returning from." He turned to the man by the door. "Now, Mr. Smith, if you would be so kind as to escort these ladies out."

Cooper grabbed Grace's arm and started to lead her across the room but she jerked it away and tore herself free. Rachel stood watching, afraid for her friend as she fought off the advancing man.

"We're not leaving with you," Grace shouted, hoping someone outside the room might hear. "You either shoot us now, or let us go."

"What about it, Mr. Smith?" Rachel yelled as she stood defiantly to face the man pointing a gun at her. "How do you feel about shooting a woman in cold blood? My father may be a blowhard but he raised his daughter to stand tall in the face of danger and not grovel to a man like you." She stuck out her chin, and waited for the reaction from John Cooper and his accomplice.

Cooper began to clap. "Excellent performance, Miss Kelly. I like a little spunk in a woman." He pulled a gun from his suit pocket and pointed it at Grace. The fun is over ladies so start walking or I'll let Mr. Smith choke the life out of you where you stand."

There was a knock and all four turned toward the direction of the door. Mr. Smith stood with his gun positioned for an intruder.

Cooper held his gun on the women and motioned for them to back up before calling out.

"Who is it?"

"This is Will from the front desk. We're going to need that room and I wanted to come in and make sure everything was ready."

"We'll be out in a moment," Cooper answered.

Grace nearly fell as he pushed her toward Rachel. They clung together, looking at each other in surprise when they recognized the voice of the desk clerk as belonging to Will Spencer. The two held hands in silence as John Cooper stood with his back to the window, his gun pointed at them and warning the two to keep quiet.

Rachel tightly squeezed Grace's hand. Her eyes darted rapidly back and forth between her friend and the window. Grace had seen it too and squeezed Rachel's hand in return. While John Cooper was distracted by the knock at the door, they got a glimpse of Griffin quickly peeking through the window from the alley. It was only for a moment as his head popped out from the side then disappeared leaving the women scared to move, mortified they would give away their secret. Grace's heart beat with trepidation. She wanted to cry out to him but couldn't. Griff had come to rescue them and her stomach fluttered with wild excitement. There was another rapid knock at the door.

"Sir, could you open the door? I wonder if I might speak to you for a moment?"

Mr. Smith looked at Cooper for instructions as John moved behind the young women and pushed his gun in Rachel's back. "Open the door," he whispered.

Mr. Smith cracked the door several inches and Will's unassuming face poked through. He scanned the room and paused when he saw John Cooper. Grace and Rachel looked at each other with wide eyes, trying to subdue a grin.

"Excuse me sir. I'm from the desk. I was wondering if you and the ladies would like some tea? I can have a tray sent in right away."

"No, thank you," Cooper said, impatiently to the supposed desk clerk. "I told you we were about to leave."

Again, Grace saw Griff's head bobbing in the corner of the window and felt she must do something to stall. She held her handbag close to her chest and tried to think of a way to give them more time. Pressed against her body, hidden in the bag, was the hard outline of the Colt 45 she had taken from the nightstand. She nonchalantly moved behind Rachel and opened her bag, slowly removing the gun and concealing it in the skirt of her dress. Wrapping her finger around the trigger, she took a deep breath, mustered her courage and hoped for a steady hand as she raised the pistol and shot at an oil lamp sitting on a table. The shattering pieces of glass exploded in the air drawing the attention of John Cooper and Mr. Smith. Rachel screamed in terror as Grace pushed her to the ground then pivoted to face Cooper. He reeled in her direction with a look of shock and took aim.

Reece Cameron burst through the door, knocking Mr. Smith to the ground. Without hesitation he shot at Cooper, hitting his firing hand, sending the gun to the floor. Griffin followed next wielding his pistol. Will Spencer appeared in the doorway holding a shotgun.

Reece approached Cooper, kicking his gun away and pulled out a set of handcuffs. Will held his gun on Mr. Smith as Griff crossed the room, helping his sister to stand. Both women wrapped their arms around him, clutching his neck.

"You and little Kelly sister alright, Grace?" asked Reece as he held Cooper's arm.

"We're fine, sheriff," Rachel snapped back with clinched teeth. "Thank you for asking."

"Grace, what were you two doing?" Griff asked. "This man is a murderer. Why would you put yourself in danger?"

"We didn't know," she replied. "He said he was Allister Neal and it wasn't until I saw him that I realized who he really was. How did you know we were here?"

"Margaret told me," said Will. "She didn't like the idea of you girls meeting a strange man in a hotel. She was suspicious from the beginning and so upset, after you left she drove the buggy straight to my office."

"I'm so sorry we worried her, Mr. Spencer," said Grace "If we had taken her advice in the first place, this never would have happened. I don't know what we were thinking. I hope Margaret can forgive us."

"Nothing to forgive, young lady. I must say, I was taken aback when Margaret rushed into my office with the news of your meeting with Mr. Neal. I haven't seen my wife that riled up in years. She had my shotgun in hand. Brought it with her from home and told me if I didn't hightail it over here to find you two then she would take the gun and come herself."

Will chucked to himself and raised the shotgun to show the others. "Can you imagine my Margaret bursting into the room brandishing this thing? She would have had these criminals hogtied and ready for the sheriff before they knew what happened."

"It would have been a sight to see, that's for sure," laughed Rachel.

"Reece and I were just getting back to town when we saw Will running across the street to the hotel, gun in hand," explained Griff. "He told us the story and once the hotel clerk verified that you were in the room, we worked up a plan to get you out."

"Will is the real hero," said Reece. "He concocted the idea of pretending to be the hotel clerk so we could get a peek in here and see what was going on. Griff went around the side to the alley in case they tried to escape that way."

"We tried that, ourselves," said Rachel. "It didn't work."

"We had you covered from the start but we wanted to avoid gunfire if we could."

"You can imagine what we thought when we heard the gun shot and someone scream," said Griff. He hugged Grace and smiled. "Shooting that lamp gave us the chance we were waiting for. You shot that thing to pieces. What were you aiming at?"

"Actually, I was aiming for the lamp. I could have shot one of the men but I was afraid the other would fire back and hit Rachel. That's why I pushed her to the ground. I wanted her out of the line of fire. I saw you outside the window and knew Will was on the other side of the door so I shot at the lamp thinking that would draw their attention long enough for you to make a move."

"You did good, Grace. You're a smart woman."

"Lamont Bannister has the deed to the ranch," said Grace. "That's what everyone has been looking for. I buried it under an old log. This whole thing was about the deed to my father's ranch."

"Lamont is dead," called Reece as he led John Cooper out the door followed by Will who held tight the Mr. Smith. "He showed up this morning at the cliffs not long after Griff and I got there. Mr. Cooper, here, is the last one left who was involved in your father's murder. He and Mr. Smith will be facing a federal judge in Carson City and it will be my pleasure to escort them on that trip."

"Pa is going to be mad when he finds out what a foolish thing you've done, Rachel. Coming here and bringing Grace with you on a harebrained plan to see Allister Neal. I thought you'd be smarter."

"It wasn't really harebrained. Even you and Reece thought Allister Neal was a legitimate businessman. How were we to know he would try to kill us?"

"Just the same, you should have waited for me."

Tom Kelly threw the door open with such force that it slammed against the wall. Stomping into the room he looked around with a wild eye. "Lance, they're in here."

"Pa," Rachel cried, running to her father. "I was so frightened."

Tom grabbed his daughter, tears filling his eyes. "I was half crazy when I got Will's message. Lance and I came as quick as we could. I thought we might have lost you."

"I'm alright. Thanks to Grace's fast thinking. She kept a cool head. I could hardly breath."

Are those the men outside with Reece? The ones being led away?" said Lance, entering the room. "Did they really think they were going to get Rachel and Grace out of this hotel without someone noticing?"

"They had us believing it, Lance," said Rachel. "John Cooper threatened to kill us right here on the spot if we said a word. He wanted to sneak us out the side door. You would have been proud of me, Pa. I never backed down when he threatened us. Even when he called you a boring old blowhard."

Lance snickered and glanced at Griffin who struggled to keep a straight face. Tom scowled at both sons then hugged his daughter again. "You did fine, little girl. I'm proud of you." He looked at Griff and smiled. "I'm proud of all my children."

"While we're all here...well, except for Matt and Elizabeth, I wanted to say something," Griff started. "I haven't had a chance to talk to Grace…I mean Anne. I've been waiting for the right time but she keeps finding ways to get herself into trouble."

He took Grace's hand and turned to face her. "Will Spencer said marriage is about finding that one person to fight life's battles with and I figure we've fought enough together to last for an eternity. I've been hoping that you feel the same way and would consent to marry me."

Rachel squealed and clapped as Griffin pulled Grace into his arms and kissed her. "I realize I haven't let you know how I feel and maybe this isn't the place but you're everything to me and I don't think the Emerald will ever mean as much if you're not there to share it."

"I've known for a long time I would never be able to leave you," answered Grace. "In fact, there were times when I didn't want to tell you my memory was coming back because I thought that would mean I'd have to go away."

"I've never cared what you remembered as long as you didn't forget me."

"I never will," Grace whispered, tears streaming down her cheeks.

"I can see how happy my son has been since he met you, Grace," said Tom as he approached the two and gave her a hug. I want you to know you're a part of the Kelly family now."

Grace put her arm through Griffin's and smiled. "You still owe me a picnic."

"I have a spot picked out for us, remember? Let's go home."

Epilogue

Griffin Kelly helped his bride down from the carriage. She held his arm while surveying the ranch and drew a sharp breath when her eyes found the burned ashes of what was once a house. They slowly walked toward the rubble, carefully stepping over bits of glass and charred wood. The stone fireplace, still standing, was a tribute to her father's skilled masonry.

"This was the parlor," she explained, pointing to an area that once was the front of the house. A soggy chair cushion lay on the ground, almost unrecognizable. "My father and I use to sit on the porch in the evening when it was warm. There was a swing at one end but that's gone now."

"We'll build it back if you want," Griffin said as he held her arm. "The house and barn. I'll build it exactly as it was before."

They moved to another spot where an old stove sat, covered with soot and ashes. Grace lovingly brushed the top with her hand, scattering the gray dust. "This stove is like the one you have. Like the one we have in our kitchen. It was the first thing I remembered when my memory started to return."

"You don't have to give it up. We can take it back with us if it will make you happy," Griff said.

"You make me happy. More so than this comfortable place I once called home. It's a memory now. One I hope I never again forget. It holds good thoughts and bad and although I will always remember the love shared here, I'll remember the sadness too."

She leaned her head on his shoulder and sighed. "I no longer want to look to the past, only the future. Our future and the life we will build together. The life I will have with my Emerald man."

"I promise to make it a good life," Griff said with a smile.

"You already have."

The End

Acknowledgments

Many thanks to those who offered their support for this, my second project, and helped to continue my dream.

About the Author

Leigh Stephens has a passion for reading and writing. For years she expressed her creativity through her work in newspapers before writing her first book. She is a native of Illinois with a degree in Communications and currently lives in Arkansas.

Did you enjoy Emerald Man, by Leigh Stephens?
Then you'll be entertained by Emerald Heart, book one of her Emerald Series.
Here's a sample of what you will find.

EMERALD HEART

LEIGH STEPHENS

CHAPTER 1

The Trip West

Nevada 1875

Elizabeth Rogers shoved her elbow into the man's side as hard as she could. His snoring momentarily ceased as he snorted and mumbled incoherently. She breathed a disgusted sigh and poked him again then pushed him off her shoulder. It had been this way since Salt Lake and she had enough.

The man opened his eyes and looked around at the other passengers on the stage then focused on Elizabeth, realizing at last that he had once again been sleeping on her shoulder. "My apologies miss," he said in a not-so apologetic voice. "It's difficult to get comfortable when the stage is rocking back and forth." He scooted his body over toward the gentleman on the other side of him who rolled his eyes and leaned as far away as he could.

She did not answer but instead looked out the window and stared. The passing landscape was soothing, and she closed her eyes for a moment thinking of the long way she'd come. Her trip began in Missouri where she grew up on a farm with her parents and older brother, Jim. He was ten years older and took charge of the farm and her welfare after their parents died in a cholera epidemic. They worked the land together. Jim spent his days in the fields and she took care of the home while still going to school. He insisted she continue her education.

When the war started, so many boys from their county joined the fight that Jim felt it was his duty to go. His regiment left for Tennessee to face the Confederates and a year later she received a letter informing her that he had been killed. The news was devastating.

Elizabeth opened her eyes when the stage jumped as it hit a rut in the road throwing the passengers into the air then slamming them back down on the hard, wooden seats. The man sitting beside her threw his arm out to catch his balance and slapped her in the face, knocking her hat sideways and crushing the brim.

"My apologies once again," he said as he righted himself. "I believe this is the most uncomfortable ride I've ever taken. Six passengers in a small coach are entirely unacceptable in my opinion."

"It's a tight squeeze that's for sure," said the gentleman sitting on the other side. "And nearly impossible when you insist on lying on top of this young lady and myself as you sleep."

"I beg your pardon," said the man indignantly as he straightened the suit jacket stretched over his bulging stomach. "I have every right to rest my eyes during this trip."

"Well, we have every right to sit in peace without listening to your snoring like a grunting hog but that doesn't seem to be the case."

The other passengers joined in the conversation with a flurry of barbs for each other as they aired their grievances. There were accusations of shin kicking, foot stomping, hip nuzzling and foul odors that lasted for the next mile until Elizabeth thought she might just open the door and jump or at least ask the driver at the next stop if she could sit up top with him. Finally, a well-dressed man sitting across from her pulled out his gun and threatened to shoot the next person who opened their mouth with a complaint. The coach fell silent as passengers leered at the gentleman and he put away his gun, pulling out a small cigar instead. He lit the end and leaned back as the puffs of smoke floated out the window. The smell of cigar smoke in such a tight space wasn't the solution Elizabeth was looking for but at least it was peaceful. She stared out the window and thought of home again.

It was impossible for her to run the ranch by herself after Jim was killed so, for a time, she lived with her aunt and uncle. They did their best to include her in their family of six, but Elizabeth missed the house she grew up in. The loss of her parents and brother was overwhelming and when her sorrow was too much to bear, her comfort came from sitting on the bank of the creek near their farm with her feet emerged in the cool running water. As a young girl, she would spend a long summer's day sticking her toes in the muddy bottom while Jim caught crawdads with his makeshift net. The old creek, with its dark swirling water, was a haven and she smiled, remembering those sweet moments of her childhood.

Alex Rogers, like Jim, fought in the war. Upon returning home, he needed employment and found it through working for Elizabeth's uncle on her farm. They met for the first time one afternoon when she sat on the banks of the little creek. He came to fish and forget the things he saw on the battlefield and she, to grieve the loss of her family.

He was a gentle man and a hard worker. Although, not especially handsome, he possessed a quick wit and the ability to make Elizabeth laugh so it was easy for her to fall in love. She wondered now if it was a love that would have sustained but he filled that empty void in her heart and she offered him the home he was looking for. They were married, and Elizabeth was sure she was destined to be happy after all. Fate, however, is sometimes cruel and just when she thought her dreams had come true, her life was torn apart once more.

Their first winter was harsh. Elizabeth couldn't remember ever seeing so much snow. The cold winds would whip over the barren fields and seemed to penetrate every seam in the walls of their home. They struggled to keep the animals fed and watered and Alex wondered if their supply of food and firewood would last until spring. Warm weather arrived, and planting season promised a good year ahead. The melting snows brought surging water and the river, with its swift moving current, swelled and spilled over into the fields.

"Next stop in ten minutes," the stage coach driver shouted down. Passengers began to wiggle in their seats and the stout man next to her tried to stretch his leg but withdrew it when the cowboy across from him cleared his throat and scowled. The gentleman with the cigar sent another puff of smoke into the air and smiled at her. She returned the smile then looked out the window again hoping to see the station in the distance.

Alex would have hated the west. He was a farm boy at heart and loved working the land and raising their stock. They were missing a calf, as she remembered. It rained for three days straight and the roads were all but washed out. Still, he wanted to go despite her worry over the danger. He needed to find that calf. The river was rising over the banks and the poor animal had gotten tangled up in brush wrapped around a fallen tree. Alex worked to free him and as he was carrying the calf up the bank to safety, he slipped and fell back into the water where the rapid undercurrent pulled him down and carried him away. Elizabeth was grief stricken. She shut herself away from everything, never leaving her house. She no longer found pleasure in her childhood home and knew she must leave the lonely place it had become. She decided to sell her farm and move far enough away to forget her sorrow and with the help of her uncle, settled on Nevada as a destination.

"The station is just ahead folks. We'll change horses and then be on our way," the driver yelled down to the coach. Elizabeth straightened her hat as best she could and waited for the stage to stop. The station master, who was a scraggly old man, opened the door and the gentleman with the cigar climbed out first then turned to offer Elizabeth his hand.

"Thank you," she said and climbed down catching the hem of her dress on the stair and tearing a portion. She gave out a dejected sigh and reached to pull it free.

"Let me get that for you," said the gentleman. He reached down and unhooked the hem from the rusty nail it was attached to. "I'm afraid it might have ruined your dress."

Elizabeth gave him a faint smile and walked into the station which was nothing more than a small cabin. It was musty inside and barely lit with a few small windows but there was a table and some chairs and the offer of a glass of water for the passengers. A meal of beans and cornbread along with hot coffee could be purchased for a dollar but after the dusty trip she had no appetite and no desire to sit so she walked outside to watch the station master change the team for the next leg of the journey.

"We should be in town by supper, if all goes well."

Elizabeth turned to see the gentleman with the cigar standing beside her. He looked to be in his late thirties and well dressed for this part of the country. He was slender with smooth dark hair and a thin mustache. She could tell his suit was expensive and he spoke with a slight drawl making him seem out of place in these parts. She was suspicious of a man like him who would attempt to befriend a young woman traveling alone and took a step backwards.

"If all goes well? I don't know how it can get much worse," Elizabeth said. "An entire day spent on this rocking, wooden box, squeezed in next to an oversized man who uses me for a pillow."

The gentleman laughed out loud with such force that it caused Elizabeth to laugh too and her distorted hat slid down the side of her head. "I was wrong," she chuckled. "My new hat is now completely ruined." She straightened it again then looked questioningly at the man. "What did you mean, if all goes well?"

"I just meant we should be on time if we don't run into trouble along the way," he said as he threw down his cigar butt and smashed it into the ground. "These roads are full of ruts and we might lose a wheel. I don't mean to scare you, but stages have been known to be robbed from time to time and there is an occasional Indian attack although I believe those have subsided drastically."

"Well, you've certainly done a good job of not scaring me," Elizabeth said sarcastically. "When does the frightening information start?"

The gentleman laughed again. "I apologize, miss," he said. "It was my intention to begin a simple conversation with the hope of passing the time and now it seems I've blundered the whole thing. Forgive me for mentioning any possible issues we may have on the last part of our journey. I have faith in the Overland Company and know that it will bring us safely to our desired destination."

Elizabeth gave him a skeptical look and thought the best course of action would be to go back to the station house until time to leave and she started to walk away.

"My name in Jack Devlin and I mean you no harm. It's just that, as you say, we've been stuck in the wooden box for many hours and I thought I might introduce myself."

"Elizabeth Rogers," she replied. "Nice to meet you, Mr. Devlin and thank you for quieting down the others during the squabbling, although your method was somewhat unusual." She smiled at the thought of the stunned passengers when he flashed his pistol.

"I have to admit they all made their point, but I wasn't about to listen to them for the rest of the trip. It's amazing how people seem to change their attitude when they're looking at the barrel end of a gun. I hope it didn't frighten you."

"Not at all, Mr. Devlin," she smiled. "I rather enjoyed it and it gave me some peace and quiet which is something I could use right now."

"Where do you come from, Miss Rogers? How is it that a young lady as pretty as you is traveling alone?"

"I'm from Missouri... just west of Saint Louis. My husband and I owned a farm there," Elizabeth replied.

"And he is minding the farm in Missouri while you travel west?"

"He was drowned several years ago in an accident," Elizabeth replied, looking away for a moment and pausing. "I'm traveling alone."

"My apologies for prying," replied Devlin. "I'm sorry for your loss. It's been a long trip for you, I'm sure."

Elizabeth took a deep breath. "It seems like it's lasted forever. I left St. Louis last week on the train for Kansas City and on to Omaha from there. Then four nights on the Union Pacific to Utah. I picked up the stage in Salt Lake. How about you, Mr. Devlin? Where did you come from?"

"I can claim a lot of places, Mrs. Rogers," said Devlin. "Most recently Denver where I was participating in a card game which lasted longer than I expected. I'm on my way to Sacramento now."

"To play in another game?"

"It is my profession and I'm very good at it. I've taken this stage because I need to make a brief stop to pick up a horse I've purchased. I'll be taking him west with me."

"Loading up," shouted the station master.

Elizabeth and Jack Devlin headed toward the stage and waited as the other passengers boarded. He held the door as she placed her foot on the stair, mindful of the rusty nail sticking out on the bottom of the step. She turned to Devlin with a serious look.

"There aren't really Indian attacks, are there?"

"No, Mrs. Rogers," he smiled. "Not today." He helped her into the coach and waited for her to sit before climbing in himself and closing the door.

CHAPTER 2

Confrontation

"Whoa," the driver called as the stage came to a halt. He climbed down and paused for a moment to stretch before opening the door of the coach. "End of the line for the day, folks. You can wait inside if you want while we unpack the luggage. The hotel is down the street to your left and Elkhorn Saloon to your right."

Jack Devlin climbed down and looked around while the station master helped Elizabeth. "Careful of the step," Devlin reminded her and she held up her dress and petticoat to avoid the nail.

Elizabeth watched the chaos on the sidewalk in front of the station depot. A man had scrambled to the top of the stagecoach and was untying the rope which held the luggage in place while another stood below ready to receive the trunks and carpetbags as they were handed down. Some of the passengers had already gone inside but the large man who sat beside her stayed and was giving directives to the young man for his things to be unloaded first.

"What are your plans now, Mrs. Rogers?" said Devlin over the noise. "May I assist in finding someone to help with your things?"

A large mail bag was thrown to the ground almost landing on Elizabeth. She scooted out of the way with a frightened look. Her hat began to slide, and she grabbed it with one hand pushing it back while moving closer to Devlin. She was just about to speak when a cowboy walked up beside her and shouted to the man on top of the coach.

"You got a saddle up there for the Emerald ranch? Suppose to be coming from Denver."

Elizabeth gave the man a disapproving look as she put her hand over her ear to shield it from his shouting. She inched toward Devlin and paused when she heard the sound of tearing fabric. Looking down, she realized the cowboy was standing on the frayed hem of her dress.

"Got it right here," the man on top yelled back. He picked up a saddle and threw it down to the cowboy who shouted back his thanks.

"Please, sir," she said in frustration as she tried to pull her dress from under the man's boot.

"What?" answered the cowboy. He turned around holding the saddle and knocked her into Jack's arms. "Sorry, ma'am," he said, then hurriedly walked over to the front of the building and dropped the saddle.

"I'm going to leave this here for my brother," the cowboy shouted to the man on top who was struggling with a large trunk. "He should be here with the wagon in a couple of minutes to pick it up. I've got some place else I need to be."

"I'll see that he gets it," said the station manager walking up from behind and slapping the cowboy on his back. "How's that boss man at the Emerald getting along?"

"Barking orders as usual," said the cowboy with a smile. "He's gone and bought his already spoiled daughter a new saddle and sent me to town to pick it up. I'm running in eight different directions."

"Well, that's why he has you, Matthew," said the station master with a grin. "You and Griffin both work hard for him as well you should. Tell him to stop by and see me the next time he's in town and I'll buy him a drink."

"I will," laughed the cowboy. "Remind Griff when he shows up that I'll meet him at the Elkhorn. I need to run."

"I can't believe..." Elizabeth said to Devlin after she composed herself. Still red-faced, she smoothed her skirt and surveyed the damage to the hem. "I'm sorry that dusty cowhand rushed off before I had the opportunity to tell him what I think. Is everyone that rude in this part of the country?"

"Mostly the younger ones," Devlin said with a grin. "Some of those cowboys spend so much time with their cows, they forget how to act around people. They're better off limiting their conversations to animals. Now, as I was saying, would you allow me to have your things removed to the hotel? I'll be staying there myself for the evening and it's no trouble."

"Oh, no thank you," Elizabeth replied. "I'm not staying at the hotel. Someone is meeting me here and taking me directly to my ranch. It's what I've come for. I sold our farm after my husband died and with the help of my generous uncle who has done everything possible to make up for the sadness in my life, I have the money to buy a ranch."

"Ranch?" said Devlin with a look of surprise. "I salute you madam on such a large undertaking for a woman alone. Do you know much about ranching?"

"Not a thing," Elizabeth laughed. "But I was raised on a farm. I know about animals and crops. How much different can a herd of cows be? My uncle insisted I hire a foreman to run things and I plan to learn from him."

"Your uncle sounds like a smart man and I salute him as well for taking such good care of you. Should I wait with you until someone arrives? I have nothing to do until tomorrow when I pick up my horse."

"You're such a kind man, Mr. Devlin. Nothing like the others I've seen so far. I'll be fine by myself. I plan to go inside and wire my uncle that I've arrived safely and I'm sure my contact will be here shortly. Much luck with your next card game in Sacramento and your new horse."

Well then," said Devlin as he reached in his vest pocket and pulled out a card, handing it to Elizabeth. "I can be reached at this address. Please contact me should you ever need assistance of any kind." He smiled as he put the card in her hand. "Should you need a sleeping gentleman forcibly removed from your shoulder or a wild cowboy cured of his rudeness, I will always be at your service."

Elizabeth smiled and said goodbye then walked inside to find the station master. She was anxious to let her Uncle know about the trip. She also wanted to find his friend, Will Spencer, who would take her to the ranch. Her spirits were high considering the day she had. She looked frightful with a dress full of wrinkles and a torn hem. The cowboy had knocked one of the combs lose in her hair which was dirty and now in danger of coming completely undone and falling to her shoulders in a tangled mess. She looked forward to a good supper and relaxing bath. Stepping up to the counter, she gave the station master her name.

"Are you Elizabeth Rogers from Missouri?" the station master asked when she inquired about Will Spencer. "He sent over a message saying he's been tied up and asked for you to meet him at his office if that was possible. It's just down the street next to the bank. I can have someone escort you over."

"That's not necessary, I'll find it myself."

This was a little disappointing, Elizabeth thought as she let out a sigh. She was hoping to leave for the ranch right away and now it seems Mr. Spencer scheduled an appointment. Well, it probably couldn't be helped. After all, a man like Will Spencer had a business to run. The walk would do her good after sitting for such a long time on the stage and she headed down the street.

Will Spencer was a friend of Elizabeth's uncle. They were acquainted years ago in St. Louis at the stock yards. Will was a financier and her uncle would take his cattle to the yards to be sold. They seemed to hit it off from the beginning and both prospered from the friendship. Will married his wife, Margaret, and moved west in the 1850's during the gold rush. He wasn't interested in prospecting. He had come to invest and settled in Nevada where silver was being discovered almost daily.

When Elizabeth made the decision to move west her uncle was frantic. How could a twenty-three-year-old, unmarried woman think about traveling across the country by herself? She would have no one to care for her. It was dangerous and completely unacceptable in her uncle's opinion. But Elizabeth made up her mind and didn't care what anyone else thought.

Out of desperation he wrote to his old friend and asked for help. Will was honored by the request. He and Margaret set about finding a ranch suitable for Elizabeth. Something with acreage to raise crops and cattle. He hired the best ranch foreman he could find and stocked the ranch with enough cattle to get started. Repairs were made on the house and buildings which were run down. Margaret took charge of the furnishings, a job she thoroughly enjoyed and made sure Elizabeth's new home would be stylish and comfortable. It was the general opinion of everyone, except Elizabeth, that she would give up the idea of owning a cattle ranch after spending some time in the rough land of Nevada, but Will and Margaret intended to make sure she had everything she needed on this end to be a success.

The door to Will Spencer's office opened with a jolt just as Elizabeth reached for the handle and the cowboy stepped through the thresh hold looking backward as he was talking to someone inside.

"Let me talk to Pa about your idea for that silver mine. He may want to include Henry Richter in this deal. I'll stop back later in the week."

He turned around to face forward and not noticing Elizabeth, slammed into her, knocking her backwards with full force. She gave out a yelp and grabbed for his arms to keep from falling as her pitiful hat slid down her head once more.

"Whoa, excuse me miss. I didn't see you there," said the cowboy as he put his hands around her waist to steady her balance and looked down, wondering why her face was familiar."

Elizabeth tore the hat from her head and glared. "You again," she shouted. "Have you no shame? It's obvious you have no manners from the way you acted at the station but now, to push your way through the door like a bull headed for the feeding trough is practically uncivilized. First you push me and tear my dress and now you've stomped on my foot. Hopefully I won't go lame." She winced as she wiggled her toes inside her shoe to make sure they were all in working order.

"Tore your dress?" Matt Kelly said doubtfully, still trying to figure out where he had seen this woman before. "This was just an accident and I said I was sorry. There's no need to get ugly."

"Ugly, now I'm ugly?" Elizabeth screeched in a high-pitched voice. "What kind of thing is that to say to a lady?"

The cowboy shook his head in exasperation. "Look Miss, I'm not calling anyone ugly." He looked around the busy street embarrassed at the confrontation with this young lady. "I didn't see you when I walked out, and I've apologized for it. Now you're raising your voice and carrying on..."

He paused for a moment as he looked at a pair of pretty blue eyes giving him a cold stare. She was a little thing, barely came to his shoulder. No wonder he didn't see her. He smiled to himself as he noticed her blonde hair loosely pinned up with something poking haphazardly from her head. What was on the end of the hairpin, a butterfly?

Elizabeth's face turned red with anger. This was the most aggravating man she had ever met. He did, indeed, push her and tear her dress and step on her foot which was hurting quite a bit right now and he couldn't understand why she was upset.

"Sir," she began. "And I question my judgment in using that term in regard to your person. I am hot and tired and can't remember the last time I had a decent meal." Tears began to well in her eyes and her voice cracked as she took a deep breath and spoke. "It's obvious you have no sense. Mr. Devlin was right. You just need to go talk to your cows." She threw her dilapidated hat at the cowboy hitting him in the face. "Now if you'll please step aside, I'm late for an appointment."

Matt turned sideways as she squeezed through the door and walked away in a huff. He bent down and picked up the crumpled straw hat decorated with light blue ribbons and straightened the bent brim, then headed down the street. What just went on there, he wondered? It's been a busy day and all he did was open a door and walk out. A woman runs into him or, on second thought, he might have run into her. It was difficult to remember with those bright blue eyes staring like you just cussed in church. Hadn't he apologized? Yes sir, he had and still, she threw a fit. Where did she come from? Did she need help? She said she hadn't eaten.

"Well if that's not a sight to behold. The pride of the Kelly family walking down the street muttering to himself?' Matt stopped in front of the Elkhorn Saloon and looked up to see his brother Griffin leaning against the side of the building. "Where have you been?"

"I just came from my meeting with Will and he wants Pa to buy into that silver mine."

"What was your answer?" Griffin asked as he pushed the door of the saloon open and walked inside looking for an empty table.

"I told her I was sorry, what else could I say?" answered Matt as the two sat down and motioned for one of the working girls to bring them a couple of beers.

Griffin stared at his brother as if he just walked into the wrong conversation. "Told who you were sorry? Where did you say you were?"

"I was coming out of Will's office and literally ran into a woman," Matt replied. "I may have stepped on her foot, but I did not rip her dress. I'm not taking the blame for that one."

Griffin sat back in his chair and grinned. His brother was completely flustered, and he was enjoying every minute of it. "So, you stepped on some woman's foot, ripped her dress, and then apologized? What about the silver mine?"

"I said we'd think about it and then she told me to go talk to my cows," Matt answered as he contemplated the conversation he had with the woman.

The saloon girl put the beers in front of the men then sat down in the empty chair. "Not now Marie," said Griffin. "This is too good." The woman gave him a disappointed look and got up to move on to another table. "Let me get this straight. Was the woman in the meeting with you and Will? Why do you need to talk to cows?"

Matt took a drink of beer and grunted as he slammed the glass down on the table. "Pay attention Griff. Why would the woman be in a meeting with me and Will? She was coming in the door and I ran into her and now she claims she is going lame and threw her hat at me." He placed the hat with blue ribbons on the table. "There it is, right there."

"Going lame?" Griffin began to laugh. "Why in the world is she going lame? I gotta tell you Matt, I think you're losing your touch. I've had women throw a lot of things at me. Some nice, some not so nice, but a hat..."

"It's not funny," Matt interrupted with a scowl. "She just threw it in my face and walked off. What kind of woman does that?"

Griffin picked up his beer and started to drink. "Was she pretty? Would I like her?"

"I guess she was. I just saw her for a moment." Matt began to think back to when the young woman looked at him in anger. "She was mad at the time and yelling that I had no sense. She had blue eyes, that's all I know...and blonde hair with a butterfly thing." He took another drink and slammed the glass down on the table again then motioned for Marie to bring them another round.

"She's got you riled up, whoever she is," said Griffin, intrigued by this woman who could make his ever so calm older brother babble on about a female this way.

"I'm not riled up. Finish your beer so we can go," Matt snapped. He was already irritated and now Griffin was beginning to annoy him. He regretted bringing it up.

"Well you could have fooled me." Griffin knew it was best to keep his mouth shut so the two sat there in silence and drank their beer. He smiled to himself, full of curiosity about the nameless girl with the blue eyes wandering the streets and the possibility that there was a woman who could best his brother.

Made in the USA
Lexington, KY
27 January 2018